Norma Clarke was bor... ...'s
Old Kent Road. As a sm... ...r.
The 188 bus, destination ... ...
she sought. For many ye... ..., when she
grew up, to ride the 188 a... ...on her first literary prize
at the age of nine – six chocolate eggs for coming third in a road
safety competition – and launched a school newspaper at the age of
fourteen.

Norma Clarke still lives in London and longs for the country. With
her husband and two sons, she escapes as often as possible to remote
parts of Northumberland and Yorkshire. Her walking boots (over
twenty years old and still going strong) are among her most prized
possessions. Her interests also include nineteenth-century literature,
on which she has written academic books and articles.

by the same author

PATRICK IN PERSON

THEO'S TIME

Patrick and the Rotten Roman Rubbish

NORMA CLARKE

Illustrated by Vanessa Julian-Ottie

faber and faber
LONDON · BOSTON

First published in 1993
by Faber and Faber Limited
3 Queen Square London WC1N 3AU

First published in paperback in 1995

Photoset by Parker Typesetting Service, Leicester
Printed in England by Clays Ltd, St Ives plc

A CIP record for this book is available from the British Library.

ISBN 0 571 17354 3

2 4 6 8 10 9 7 5 3 1

for Lynette,
who is interested in everything

Contents

1   Beginning with the Romans

It all started with a loose tooth. Or perhaps it all started when my brother Jack brought a book home from school called *Augustus Caesar's World*. Jack was very interested in the Romans. I was very interested in my loose tooth.

We were sitting round the table in the kitchen, eating dinner. Well, the others were all eating dinner. I was staring miserably at my plate and rocking my loose tooth backwards and forwards with my tongue.

'It's getting looser and looser,' I said.

Nobody took any notice.

'I expect it'll fall out soon,' I said.

Nobody answered.

'I can't eat,' I said.

'Nobody cared. Only Big Dog, sitting in my lap, looked at me sadly. And he didn't have any teeth.

Mum and Dad were reading the newspaper and Jack had his nose in *Augustus Caesar's World*. Jack's teacher, Mrs Ross, said he could take it home for the whole of the summer holiday if he would stop telling her everything he knew about the Romans.

I watched my dad eating. I watched him chewing.

'What's it like?' I asked him.

'What?' he mumbled.

'Eating,' I said glumly. 'What's it like?'

I hadn't eaten one thing the whole day. Not one thing. I'd *looked* at a lot of food.

Mum said, 'When it comes out, we'll put it under your pillow. And the nice tooth fairy will come and collect it and leave you something nice in its place.'

'The nice tooth fairy?' I said.

'Yes,' Mum said cheerfully. 'The nice tooth fairy.'

'I'm seven-and-a-bit,' I had to remind her. 'Not three.'

I was too old for the *nice* tooth fairy. I was too old to have a loose tooth. In my class, everybody's teeth had fallen out when they were six.

Jack said, 'When my tooth fell out, the nice sweet runny honey mummy tooth fairy didn't put *anything* under *my* pillow.' Jack was eight-and-a-half. His teeth fell out when he was five.

Gently I pushed my tooth as far forward as it would go and then, carefully, with the tip of my tongue, I brought it back. It was very, very loose.

I let Dad look at it. 'I could pull it out for you, if you like,' he said.

'I don't like,' I said. I closed my mouth fast, pressing my lips firmly together.

'You could tie a string around it,' said Jack, throwing Augustus Caesar down and getting very interested in my tooth. 'And tie the other end to the door and slam it shut hard. That's what people used to do.'

'No, they didn't,' Dad said.

'Miss Simms says you should never do that, it's dangerous,' I told Jack, quickly jumping out of my dad's lap, out of Jack's reach. That was when I started it. That was when I made a little mistake.

Jack's book was lying on the floor, open. It was open at a big colour picture. I hopped round the other side of the book. I pointed to the picture. I said, 'Oh, look. Look at that.'

It worked. They all forgot about my tooth. They all looked at the picture.

'What is it?' said Mum, leaning sideways to get a better look.

'It's a wall the Romans built,' Jack said. 'It's Hadrian's Wall. And I really, really want to go there.'

'What's Hadrian's Wall?' That was all I said. Mum and Dad looked at each other sharply. I knew that look. It was the look they had when

they were up to something. But I didn't have time to think about what it might mean, because suddenly everybody started moving.

Dad jumped to his feet. He reached up to our corner cupboard – the one where we keep old cardboard models, empty jam jars with dried-out paint in them, tubes of glue without any lids, and useful things like that.

I looked at Mum. She was jiggling from side to side and smiling at the back of Dad's head in a secret, excited sort of way.

'Hadrian's Wall?' Dad said, throwing open the cupboard. 'It's funny you should be interested in that.'

The cardboard models, the jam jars, the glue, were all gone. The cupboard was neatly stuffed with books and big brown envelopes. They were all piled tidily, one on top of the other. Dad pulled them out.

'Roman Britain,' he said, tipping it all on the table.

Jack said, 'Wow!' and gaped.

I just gaped.

Dad pulled out a thick book and handed it to Jack. Mum pulled out a postcard and handed it to me.

'Hadrian's Wall,' Jack murmured dreamily, happily.

'Who is this Hadrian?' I said. I didn't like the

sound of him. 'What's so special about his wall?'

Something funny was going on. I didn't know what it was. But my mum and dad were definitely up to something. I put down the postcard. I had to watch them very carefully.

'Hadrian's Wall is the wall the Romans built in the north of England,' Mum said, sounding just like Jack. Her eyes were shining. 'To keep the barbarians at bay.'

Dad nodded hard. 'You'll love it,' he cried.

'And the wall is still there,' Mum said. 'And you can walk on it. Look.'

Mum picked up *Augustus Caesar's World* and showed me a soldier walking along a wall. 'Isn't this exciting!' she said. 'You can do just what that soldier did, two thousand years ago: you can walk on the wall.'

Walk on a wall? That didn't sound very exciting to me. We had a wall of our own in the garden which we could walk on if we wanted to walk on a wall.

'You can see the very things the Romans saw when they were marching up and down!' said Mum.

'You can guard the wall against the barbarian hordes,' said Dad, waving his arms about like a great flapping eagle. 'Imagine! The Roman Empire depends on you. You're a Roman soldier . . . '

'No, I'm not,' I said.

'Imagine, darling,' Mum cried.

Dad jumped up on to a chair. 'Imagine this is the wall!' he said, meaning the kitchen chair.

I shook my head sadly.

'You stand there in rain and ice and sleet and snow!' Dad cried. He put his hand to his forehead, like a sailor looking for land. 'Wind whips your face blue. Your feet are frozen, your hands are frozen, ice comes out of your nose when you blow it. In the distance you see . . . '

Mum shook her head. 'No, darling,' she said. 'The sun is shining and the sky is blue.'

'See what?' Jack asked with a big grin. 'What do you see?'

Dad got down from the chair.

'Lots of things,' he mumbled.

'What?'

I looked hard at the pictures spread out over the table. I couldn't see any of the things I really liked.

'On this wall,' I said slowly, pointing to a browny, snowy picture with browny, snowy sheep looking browny and snowy and cold in it, 'do you see things like tea-shops and cafés?'

'No,' Mum admitted.

I liked tea-shops and cafés. She liked tea-shops and cafés, too.

'Sweetshops?'

7

'No,' she said, more sharply. Jack liked sweetshops, and so did I.

'Do you see toyshops?'

'Not exactly,' Mum said. 'Though there are rather a lot of gift shops these days.'

Mum and Dad didn't like gift shops. I liked gift shops. So did Jack. We liked buying things in gift shops. I liked buying pencils with rubber dinosaurs on the end, or note-books with pictures of castles on them.

'Well, what do you see?' I asked impatiently.

I was starting to get the feeling that Mum and Dad wanted to go to Hadrian's Wall. They had been plotting it and planning it and they wanted me to want to go there with them.

'You might see interesting things like this,' Dad said. 'If you're lucky.'

He showed me a picture of a broken flower pot.

'That's nice,' I said. I looked at him closely. 'But we've got plenty of things like that in our garden. Near the wall.'

'Not exactly,' he said patiently. 'This is Roman. And this. And this.'

He showed me lots of other broken, rubbishy things. 'These are Roman treasures. Found near Hadrian's Wall.'

Mum showed Dad a broken flower pot in another book. He liked it. They started telling

8

each other how interesting the Romans were and what exciting treasures they buried in the ground.

'Jack?' I said.

'Did you know,' Jack said excitedly, 'Hadrian's Wall is seventy-three miles long!'

I knew what was coming next. 'I've got a loose tooth!' I cried.

'Roman legionaries,' Jack said, 'marched twenty miles a day with packs on their backs. Did you know the Romans built straight roads?'

'Yes,' Mum and Dad both said excitedly.

They smiled happily at Jack.

I sighed. Everybody was interested in the Romans except me. I decided to try to get interested. 'Why did the Romans build straight roads?' I asked Jack.

'So that they could march on them, of course.'

'Why?'

'Because they were Romans, of course. That's what Romans did. If you were a Roman, that's what you would do.'

'Not if I had a loose tooth,' I muttered, but under my breath.

'Well, boys,' Dad said, shuffling the Roman rubbish into a putting-away-for-now heap. 'What we thought was this. As you're so interested in the Romans, and as *we're* interested in the Romans, wouldn't it be a good idea to have a sort of Roman holiday this holiday? For a change?'

'You never know what you might find,' Mum added quickly. 'People are always turning up Roman coins, silver goblets, things that have been buried in the ground for thousands of years.'

I said, 'But I'm not interested in the Romans.'

'Oh, Patrick,' said my mum, 'I'm disappointed in you. I thought you would be interested in the Romans. Everybody's interested in the Romans, especially children.'

'Are they? Why?'

'Look,' Dad said. 'We got this from the museum shop especially for you.'

He pulled out two sheets of cardboard from the pile. He gave them to me. On one sheet was a big black-and-white drawing of a Roman man in his underwear. On the other were little drawings of different sorts of clothes. All the clothes had tags on them.

'You can colour in the clothes,' Dad said. 'Then you can cut them out and hang them on the man with these little tags.'

'You can dress him in different outfits,' said Mum. 'Hours of happy fun.'

Before I could say anything, Jack snatched the undressed Roman and tossed him aside. 'We haven't got time for any of that,' he cried. 'Not if we're going to walk Hadrian's Wall.' He stood up. 'We have serious planning to do.'

We all stared at him. At last Mum said, 'Well, not the *whole* of Hadrian's Wall, darling.'

Jack looked astonished. 'But you said!'

'No, I didn't. We can't walk the whole of it.'

'Why not? The Romans did.'

'We can't possibly. Think of Patrick.'

'Patrick's little legs can't walk seventy-three miles,' Dad said.

Mum and Dad both smiled at me in a soppy sort of way. They pointed to my legs, soppily.

'Who's calling my legs little?' I said, standing up beside Jack. My legs were only a bit shorter than Jack's. I was better at running and jumping and climbing and walking than Jack was, even if I wasn't very interested in the Romans. 'If the Romans did it, then so can I.'

Mum looked at me kindly. 'No,' she said. 'They were Roman soldiers, dear, and trained. We're just people. It's different. You can't possibly walk seventy-three miles.'

Jack's eyes glittered. 'He could if he was trained,' he said.

'Yes,' I said, thumping my fist on the table. 'Why not? Who says I can't?'

'We'll start tomorrow,' Jack declared. He fished about under the maps and books on the table until he found *Augustus Caesar's World*. He closed it with a snap and popped it under his arm. 'If anybody wants me,' he announced, 'I'll be upstairs in my quarters.'

He turned smartly on his heel and marched out of the room.

Mum and Dad sat staring, with their mouths hanging open. We all listened to the clump, clump, clump of Jack's feet as he stomped upstairs like a small army.

'Now what have we started?' Dad sighed.

'That wasn't what we had in mind at all,' Mum said in a small voice.

'How far is seventy-three miles?' I asked. 'Is it very far?' I had a loose tooth. And there was something else that was worrying me. 'This wall,' I said to Mum and Dad. 'Hadrian's Wall. Is it in Yorkshire?'

They both shifted uncomfortably.

'Not exactly,' Dad said.

I looked at them both very sternly. Now I really knew what they were getting up to. They were getting out of going to Yorkshire.

I sat back and folded my arms. 'When are we going to Yorkshire?' I demanded.

2 Sam

Yorkshire meant Jessie's house. Jessie's house meant Sam. Sam meant happiness.

Jessie was our friend who had a big house in Yorkshire that she was turning into a centre where people could come to learn things like rock climbing and abseiling and finding wild flowers in the pouring rain, which is the sort of thing people in Yorkshire like doing quite a lot.

Sam was a dog who used to stay with her sometimes and now lived with her all the time.

Mum and Dad and Jack and me were people who used to stay with Jessie sometimes. Jessie wanted us to go and live with her always. She wanted us to help run the Centre. Mum and Dad were thinking about it.

When we stayed with Jessie, Mum and Dad helped by working on the house. Jack helped by looking after Sam. I helped by keeping out of the way and by climbing up the climbing wall. Climbing and abseiling were things I liked doing quite a lot. I liked acting, too. And running. And doing backward somersaults. And eating.

I liked eating cheese and tomato sandwiches. I didn't like eating meat.

I liked being in the country and having a river, and trees, and a climbing wall, and a dog.

Jack liked being in the country, and having a dog, and reading about the Romans, and knowing a lot of things to tell people about.

Sam was the only dog Jack had in all the world. Jack loved Sam. Sam loved Jack. I loved Sam. He was our friend. Jack used to lie awake at night wishing for a dog, and when we went to Yorkshire his wishes came true.

Jack couldn't forget Sam. Jack couldn't.

It was hard to believe Jack could be so interested in the Romans and Augustus Caesar's world, that he could forget about Sam and Sam's world.

But Jack wouldn't listen to anything I tried to say to him. All he would talk about was the Romans.

In bed that night I lay in my bunk with Big Dog. Jack was talking to himself. He had a torch and a notepad and a pencil. I could hear him scribbling furiously.

'What are you writing?' I asked him.

'Nothing. Go to sleep.'

He bounced as he talked, making the springs squeak. I prodded him through his mattress.

'Jack,' I whispered. 'I can't start training yet. I've got a loose tooth.'

He didn't answer. 'Drilling and digging,' I heard him mutter. 'Pickaxe. Sickle. Bucket. Hmm. I need a mule.'

'Jack,' I said. 'I'm not sure I really want to be trained.'

'It's too late to back out now,' he grunted.

'Can't we train someone else?'

'Who?'

I thought. My friend Anna wouldn't want to be trained to be a Roman soldier. She was already training to be an actress. None of my friends in school was very interested in the Romans or in training. Then I had an idea.

'What about Alexander?' I said. 'He needs lots of training.'

Alexander, my next-door neighbour, wasn't very clever. We could probably start training Alexander without even telling him. He would never find out.

Jack wasn't listening. 'Cohorts,' he mumbled. 'Legions. Barbarians. Centurions.'

That was settled then. Jack could train Alexander. I turned over, drew my knees up and shoved Big Dog down so that his back legs rested on my knees. I pulled the quilt over us both. My tooth was still wobbling loosely in my gum. I gave it a gentle push. It was hard not to. It didn't hurt, it was just loose.

Poor tooth. Soon it would fall out and

everything would be different.

I rocked it backwards and forwards with my tongue. I closed my eyes. Perhaps my tooth would fall out. Perhaps the tooth fairy would come tonight. Perhaps my wishes would come true, too.

I opened my eyes. The room was dark. I could hear Jack breathing the way he breathed when he was fast asleep. But I wasn't scared. I was too old to believe in a tooth fairy.

A shadow crept up the wall. I closed my eyes.

I opened my eyes. Something was coming towards me.

I leapt out of bed. Shivering, blinking, clutching Big Dog, I tore down the stairs. I burst into the kitchen. My dad was standing by the cooker, holding the kettle in one hand and a cup in the other. I threw my arms around his middle.

'Don't let the tooth fairy get me!' I sobbed.

At exactly that moment, something sharp fell against the inside of my lip. I choked and spat. Dad patted me on the back with the kettle. 'Spit it out,' he said calmly.

I spat as hard as I could into his shirt. I spat and coughed till Dad said, 'I think that's probably enough, don't you?'

Slowly and carefully, I opened my eyes. My dad's shirt looked a mess. In my hand, resting in a pool of spit and blood, was my tooth. Small

and bone-coloured, a bit of me.

Mum said, not looking at my tooth at all, 'Oh lovely, darling. It's come out at last. Let's get rid of it, shall we?'

Poor fallen-out tooth. 'It's not an it, it's my tooth,' I told her. But the words sounded peculiar, like someone speaking from the bottom of the bath.

After we all rinsed my mouth out, I felt better. I sat down and had a bowl of raspberry ice-cream with raspberry jelly and tinned raspberries and raspberry yoghurt to cheer me up. I quite like raspberries.

I put my tooth on the table in front of me and told my mum and dad I was going to put it under my pillow, so that I could have a wish. 'But,' I said firmly, 'I don't want any tooth fairy taking it away.' I was going to look after it.

They said, 'Fine. What's your wish?'

I said, 'That's between me and the tooth fairy.'

Then I told them.

Early next morning Jack woke me up to start training. 'Dawn already,' Jack announced, pulling back the curtains.

It was time to start foraging.

Foraging was what the Romans did when they wanted breakfast. And dinner. And tea. And a little snack.

It was the sort of thing I liked doing, too.

We started foraging in the fridge. Then we foraged in the bread bin and in the cupboard. We foraged yoghurts, buns, biscuits, and packets of cheesey snacks.

'Jack,' I said, when all the food was finished and there was nothing left to forage. 'Jack, there's something you've forgotten.' It was time to make Jack listen.

Jack looked up from *Augustus Caesar's World*.

'Don't you remember?' I asked him.

'What?'

I looked hard at Jack.

'We promised Sam,' I said. I couldn't believe Jack could forget. 'We promised him faithfully. We crossed our hearts and hoped to die horribly. We shook paws. We promised him, rain or shine, nothing would ever stop us going to Yorkshire.'

Jack frowned and bit his lip.

'Hadrian's Wall isn't in Yorkshire,' I reminded him, just to be sure. 'Mum and Dad want to go to Hadrian's Wall. And if we go to Hadrian's Wall, we won't see Sam. And he'll miss us. He'll be sad.'

I blinked. Sam's sweet Sammy face swam in front of me. When I thought about Hadrian's Wall, all I saw was Sam with his tongue hanging out.

'Jack, we have to forget all this Hadrian's Wall Roman rubbish. We have to go to Yorkshire and make Sam happy.'

Jack said, 'Or we could take Sam to Hadrian's Wall! Sam would like to learn about the Romans.'

'We could teach him!'

We talked about Sam for a long time. Jack said, 'Sam must know a lot about the Romans already. Think how many Romans were in Yorkshire!'

'We can do Romans in Yorkshire,' I said. I wasn't sure I really wanted to do Romans in Yorkshire.

Jack told me a lot of things about Romans in Yorkshire.

Then I said, 'Jack, do you think Mum and Dad will ever decide to go and live in Yorkshire?'

Jack didn't answer. He was looking for a picture to show me.

I thought about Jessie.

Jessie said Mum and Dad were the sort of people who were always thinking about things and never doing them. Jessie was always doing things. She wasn't like other people we knew.

Not many people we knew had a climbing wall up one side of their house. Not many people we knew wanted us to go and live with them for ever and ever, but Jessie did.

That afternoon Jack had to go to the dentist. So

did Dad. It was strange that Jack had to go to the dentist when I was the one who had the loose tooth that fell out. Mum wouldn't explain. She just said, 'If you don't understand, I can't explain it to you.'

She was busy doing what she called a quick clear round. She had a big black dustbin bag in one hand and the vacuum cleaner in the other.

'When are we going to Yorkshire?' I asked.

'Out of my way,' she hissed.

She was in a hurry to get upstairs and start complaining. I followed.

Mum always complained about our bedroom. She didn't understand that the floor was a place for keeping things.

'How am I supposed to vacuum this?' she complained.

We both stood in the doorway and looked. I tried to be helpful and think how she could do it.

'When are we going to Yorkshire?' I said.

She rustled her bag and bent down. She picked up a large ball of fluff with a small, fluffy, purple bumble bee hanging on to it.

'Rubbish,' she said, popping him into the bag before I could stop her.

'No!' I cried. 'That's not rubbish.' I flung myself into the dustbin bag. I managed to get hold of the little purple bumble bee by his one wing and rescue him. It was King Beezy.

King Beezy was one of our oldest friends. He was very dusty now. I brushed his little round head and blew some specks off his tail and gently stroked the side where his other wing used to be.

'For goodness sake,' Mum cried. She threw down the bag. She unplugged the vacuum cleaner. 'I haven't got time to argue with you.'

She shoved the vacuum cleaner back in its cupboard and slammed the double door shut. It popped open. It always popped open. She grabbed her jacket and went downstairs. 'Come on,' she said.

I followed. 'Where are we going?'

She didn't answer. She was searching her pockets for her keys.

'Where's your jacket?' she said to me.

'Why?'

'So you can put it on, of course.'

'Why?'

She found her keys. They were under a pair of Jack's socks which were on the notepad which was chained up to the telephone which was on the dresser. She started marching out of the house.

'Wait for me!' I cried. 'I haven't got my jacket. Where are we going?'

In our house the passage at the bottom of the stairs is quite short and narrow. So when Mum changed her mind about hurrying and stopped dead at the front door with her hand on the latch at exactly the moment I dived from the fifth step because she told me to hurry, we crashed.

'Patrick!' she yelled, as if it were my fault.

'Well, why did you stop?' I said, after I got my breath back.

Mum couldn't remember why she stopped. She frowned. Then, 'Oh yes! I had an idea!' she cried, and pushed past me to go up the stairs again.

I stayed where I was. It was safer that way.

A moment later, Mum came down. She was nodding her head as if she was pleased with herself, and she was putting something into her shoulder bag.

3 Lies, Romans, and a Big Surprise

I still didn't know where we were going.

By the time I found out, it was too late to scream or cry or grizzle or groan or pretend I had an earache. I had no choice.

I was forced to go with Mum to somewhere called the Roman Britain Living History Society. Someone called Miss Fox was going to give us some tips about visiting Hadrian's Wall and seeing what the Romans saw.

'I'm not forcing you,' Mum said. 'But this is the only time Miss Fox is free.'

'Other children,' she said, when I doubled over in the street clutching my stomach and howling with pain, 'would give their right arms to meet a living, breathing archaeologist.'

'What's an archaeologist?' I breathed with my last breath.

'Someone who digs.' Mum yanked my hand and pulled me along behind her.

After a bit, I dried my eyes and snivelled, 'Can we go to the ice-cream parlour after?'

'We'll see.'

I was very interested in ice-cream. 'Can we?'

She said what she always said: 'If you're a good boy, we might.'

She wouldn't say anything else about the ice-cream parlour.

We were soon at the Roman Britain Horrible History Society. We went upstairs to find Miss Fox. 'Remember,' Mum hissed in my ear as she knocked at a door, 'be a good boy.'

A moment later, the door swung open and Miss Fox appeared. She had glasses, just like one of the dinner ladies at school, with wings like a butterfly. But she was bigger than the dinner lady, and more cheerful, and she blinked more and talked more. I stood still, like a good boy, watching Miss Fox blinking and talking, but I was thinking about dinner. At least, I was thinking about ice-cream.

Then I heard Miss Fox say, 'Children always *adore* the Romans! Do your children adore the Romans?'

Mum said, 'Oh yes, they do, they do!'

What! I goggled at my mum.

My mum told a lie! Just like that. She opened her mouth and a big lie popped out.

Miss Fox led Mum to a glass case. 'I must show you this,' she said.

I stayed where I was. I didn't adore the Romans. I didn't want Miss Fox to think I adored the Romans. I wasn't going to tell a lie. I folded my arms and thought about nice things like Yorkshire and Sam and ice-cream and people who didn't tell lies.

Mum called out, 'Come and see this, Patrick. Miss Fox found it herself!'

I took one step and then stood still. All this Roman Britain Living History meant Hadrian's Wall. The only wall I was interested in was Jessie's Wall.

'It's a Roman cup!' Mum cried.

'Half a Roman cup,' Miss Fox corrected her.

Half a cup? That didn't sound very exciting. What use was half a cup?

'I don't believe you,' I said.

'Imagine finding a whole half a Roman cup yourself! Just think,' Mum went on, beaming at Miss Fox, 'one day, Miss Fox might find the other half!'

Miss Fox laughed happily.

'Or she could save up and buy herself a whole one,' I grumbled.

'Patrick,' Mum said, in a warning voice.

'You told a lie!' I reminded her.

Miss Fox led my mum off to the other side of the room. They started looking at heaps of books. Mum took a book out of her shoulder bag. I watched as Miss Fox flicked through it the way my teacher Miss Simms flicked through a book to

26

find one special page. I saw her pointing, just the way Miss Simms pointed.

After a bit, Miss Fox put the book down on the pile and opened a drawer. She was searching for something. Probably another book. I thought Miss Fox was the sort of person who enjoyed searching for things and she could take a long time doing it. She wouldn't notice other people who were standing about, waiting.

I coughed and shuffled my feet. Without meaning to, just by shuffling a little bit this way and a little bit that way, I found myself standing in front of the glass case where the precious half a cup was.

It wasn't a cup at all. It was something like a piece of broken flower pot. It was dusty, honey coloured, cracked all over and had two jagged edges. In front was a card. I read it. It said: FOUND BY HENRIETTA FOX, MCMLXXVIII.

I stuck my tongue out at it.

Mum came hurrying over. She put something into my hands. 'Miss Fox was sure you would enjoy reading this,' she said. Then she hurried away. Miss Fox had some more dusty, broken bits of old flower pots to find and show her.

I looked at what Miss Fox was sure I would like. A comic. That was good. I sat down on the floor and opened it.

That was bad. It wasn't a comic at all. It was a

pretend comic. It wasn't funny. It was something about the Romans and it was pretending to be a comic so that children would think it was funny and start reading it.

It wasn't fair. I tossed it aside. Then I picked it up again. I had nothing else to do.

'Marcus lives in Rome,' I read. There was a picture of Marcus living in Rome. 'But now Marcus is coming to England.' There was a picture of Marcus on a big ship. 'Marcus is helping Caesar defend Hadrian's Wall against the barbarians.' There was a picture of Marcus standing on a wall, wearing a skirt and holding a spear.

Marcus was cold and unhappy. Marcus came from a hot country and he had never seen snow until it fell on his head on Hadrian's Wall. Poor Marcus.

I looked at the back to see if there was a big picture of Marcus in his underwear for me to cut out. There wasn't.

Poor Marcus. He probably wanted to go to Yorkshire, too. Probably he thought he *was* going to Yorkshire. Probably someone told *him* some lies.

Mum and Miss Fox were marching towards me. Miss Fox was saying, 'Not interested in the Romans . . . !'

Mum was saying, 'My other son. He's at the dentist. He's very . . . '

I stood up quickly.

'Not interested in the Romans?' Miss Fox boomed at me, blinking.

'Not very,' I mumbled. I didn't dare look up. I wished I *was* interested in the Romans. I wished I was Jack. Or Jack was me. Or I was at the dentist.

My mum started to explain to Miss Fox that I was very young and very backward.

'And you see,' she finished off, 'we all want to go to Hadrian's Wall, but all Patrick wants to do is go to Yorkshire.'

She said it in the way you might say, 'All Patrick wants to do is sit and pick his nose.'

I felt myself starting to go hot all over. Why did my mum have to say things like that?

Miss Fox made a strange huffing sound. I looked at my mum. She looked at Miss Fox.

'Is something the matter?' Mum cried in alarm.

Miss Fox closed her eyes and took a deep breath.

'Let me fetch you some water,' Mum said.

Miss Fox opened her eyes and started blinking very fast behind her spectacles.

'It's Yorkshire,' was all she would say in a mournful voice.

'Yorkshire! What about Yorkshire?' I said eagerly. Perhaps Miss Fox wasn't so bad after all.

'Are you fond of going there, too?' Mum asked her kindly.' 'Of course, there were a lot of

Romans in Yorkshire, weren't there? As well as all those barbarians. Did you find your cup in Yorkshire?'

'Yorkshire,' Miss Fox said sadly. 'Don't speak to me about Yorkshire.'

Miss Fox was blinking faster than ever. Her eyelashes were going up and down faster than a hummingbird's wings.

Mum nudged me and started to put her jacket on. 'We mustn't overtire you,' she said to Miss Fox. 'You've been terribly kind and terribly helpful. You've given us so many useful hints for our trip. But we mustn't take up any more of your time.' She started pushing me towards the door.

I slipped under her hand. 'Why don't you want people to speak to you about Yorkshire?' I asked Miss Fox.

'We're going now, Patrick,' said my mum.

'What's wrong with Yorkshire?' I said.

Miss Fox glared at me, suddenly fierce. 'I'll tell you what's wrong with Yorkshire!'

She marched off.

'Come on, Patrick,' Mum whispered. 'I think she might be batty. These people sometimes are. Too much sun. Come on. Let's go.'

'No!' I whispered back.'

Before Mum could get hold of me, Miss Fox came back. She was waving a piece of paper.

'This,' she said, holding the piece of paper as far away from her as she could, 'is what's wrong with Yorkshire!'

Mum smiled kindly at Miss Fox and scowled at me.

She took the piece of paper from Miss Fox's hand. It was a letter. I caught a glimpse of the writing. It was big and squiggly with lots of loops and swirls. The words covered the whole sheet in an untidy but interesting-looking way.

I knew the writing. I had seen it somewhere before. Where?

Mum took one look and shrieked.

She had to put her hand to her mouth to stop herself shrieking again.

'What is it, Mum?'

Mum held the letter down so I could see it. She held it out stiffly, both hands clutching the greeny-white paper so hard it crumpled.

I looked closely. All the paper was covered with scrawly writing, and all around the edges someone had drawn a nice flock of little woolly grey sheep who were all nibbling at tufts of grass.

'Look at the address,' Mum croaked.

I read it out loud. 'The Old Vicarage, Ugglemarsby, Near Igglemoor, Yorkshire.'

I stared at Mum. Mum stared at me.

Miss Fox said, 'Read the rest. This is the sort of

nonsense I've been getting from Yorkshire. All I want to do is a little dig. Most people are thrilled when I tell them they might have Roman remains on their land. Not this person. I think she's probably mad. Quite, quite mad. What do you think?'

Mum just stared at me. She wasn't listening. Suddenly I understood. Suddenly I knew where I'd seen that writing before. 'Jessie!' I cried. 'It's Jessie's writing. That's Jessie's house! How does Miss Fox know Jessie? Jessie isn't interested in the Romans!'

I snatched the letter out of my mum's hands. 'What does she say about Sam?' I cried. 'Does he miss us? Are we going to see him? Does this mean we're going to Yorkshire?'

What a tooth fairy! What quick work!

We took Miss Fox to the ice-cream parlour and Mum told her all about Jessie. Mum explained that Jessie wasn't mad – or at least, not *mad* exactly. Jessie just wasn't quite like other people. While Mum explained, I ate a few ice-creams to celebrate. I ate a Sudden Strawberry Surprise and a Tastebud Teaser for myself. Then I ate two Mission Impossibles for the tooth fairy.

Mum was explaining so hard she didn't notice. The more Mum told Miss Fox about Jessie, the less Miss Fox seemed to understand.

'Jessie has always been interested in everything,' Mum said wearily. 'And she's very kind. I'm sure this is a misunderstanding. I'm sure if I write to her and explain . . . '

'Would you?' Miss Fox beamed.

'Or even go and tell her myself . . . ' Mum tapped her spoon on the side of her dish and thought.

'Would you?' Miss Fox looked as if she couldn't believe her luck.

'Of course we would!' I told her. Mum was miles away, frowning and thinking.

Of course we would go to Jessie's house. We would forget all about Hadrian's Wall and we would go to Jessie's house and see Sam and find some buried treasure.

'Wait till I tell Jack!' I cried. 'Miss Fox,' I said happily. 'You should meet my brother Jack. He's really interested in the Romans.'

4   Buried Treasure

I held hands with Mum and we ran all the way home.

We burst through the front door, panting.

'We have to go to Yorkshire!' I yelled. 'Forget Hadrian's Wall. There's buried treasure!'

I seized a chair next to Jack and sat on it.

'Solid gold, Jack!' I cried. 'Bricks made of solid gold!'

'Jack,' I said, trying to speak and breathe at the same time. 'Something really interesting has happened about the Romans.'

Dad came down from upstairs. He wanted to know what all the slamming and banging was about.

Mum said, 'The most amazing thing has happened. You'll never guess.'

'In that case, you'd better tell me at once,' he said.

He didn't sound very excited. He didn't sound as if he really wanted to know.

'Wait till you hear, Dad!' I told him. 'You should have been there! You should have been there, Jack! There's buried treasure!'

'Buried treasure!' Jack said.

Jack wanted to know about it. Buried treasure was the sort of thing Jack liked a lot.

'Not treasure exactly,' Mum said.

'Gold is treasure!' I exclaimed. 'Bricks made of solid gold.'

Mum laughed.

'On Jessie's land!' I said. 'Jack, just think. We've been walking on top of buried treasure. Buried Roman treasure.'

'Buried treasure!' Jack said again. His eyes were goggling.

'Treasure, Dad,' I said. 'Right under our feet at Jessie's house. Roman treasure. Miss Fox said. Miss Fox knows. She had a letter. She showed us a map. She wants to dig. Under the ground. The third tree. Forty paces. But Jessie won't let her and . . . '

Mum told me to pipe down. She told me just to shut up for a minute.

'Broken pots,' I said. 'Vases. Coins. Helmets. Shields. All the things you like. But best of all is, Miss Fox said if . . . '

'Patrick!' Mum yelled. 'Stop babbling!'

I stared at her in astonishment. 'I'm not babbling,' I said. 'I'm explaining.'

Mum wanted to explain. She thought Dad would understand better if she explained.

'But I heard everything too!' I protested.

'You don't understand, Patrick.'

'Yes, I do!'

Dad sighed. 'I thought it was settled. I thought we were going to Hadrian's Wall.'

'Wait till I tell you,' Mum said eagerly.

'I wasn't babbling.'

'Be quiet, Patrick,' Dad said. 'I'm trying to listen.'

'And I'm trying to tell you!' I told him.

Mum carried on talking.

It wasn't fair. I heard everything Miss Fox said to Mum. I could tell Dad everything. I wanted to tell Dad everything but Dad didn't want to listen to me. He wanted to listen to Mum. Babbling.

I sniffed. Then I sniffed again, harder.

Mum handed me a tissue. 'It's time you learnt to blow your nose,' she said.

'Blow downwards,' Dad said.

I sniffed. Upwards.

'Patrick!' they both said.

Jack suddenly leapt to his feet and started marching up and down the kitchen, frowning hard. He had his hands behind his back. He was thinking.

I picked up Big Dog and we marched and thought with him.

'Buried treasure?' he said.

'In Jessie's garden.'

We marched and thought some more.

'Roman treasure?'

'Roman,' I said. 'A Roman temple. On Jessie's land.'

'Where?'

'Somewhere near a tree.'

'And you know how many paces?'

'Miss Fox knows.'

'And the direction?'

'Yes.'

'Good.'

We marched up and down.

'For goodness sake!' Mum babbled. 'Go into the garden if you want to do that. The whole kitchen is shaking!'

'The whole kitchen is babbling,' I muttered, but under my breath.

We sat on the low wall at the end of our garden and I told Jack everything I heard Miss Fox tell Mum.

There was lots to tell.

'It's a Roman temple,' I told him. 'Miss Fox had a picture. She showed me what it looked like.'

Miss Fox's picture was beautiful. It was more beautiful than any of the pictures in Jack's book, but I didn't tell him that. In Miss Fox's picture, the sky was blue, the grass was green, and the sun was shining. The temple was white and gold. It had lovely high white pillars at the front and a beautiful, round gold roof. Some beautiful women wearing white and gold nightdresses were scattered around, holding up trays of candles.

'And it's under Jessie's garden,' I said. 'Miss Fox knows how to dig it up, and she wants to dig it up, and Jessie won't let her.'

Jessie was a strange person.

'We could dig it up for her,' Jack said thoughtfully.

We thought about that.

'We could do it at night,' Jack said.

'I expect the Romans were good at digging,' I said. I was getting very interested in the Romans.

'The Romans were good at everything,' Jack said.

'They were good at building beautiful temples.'

'And roads.'

'And walls,' I said.

'Hadrian's Wall,' Jack said sadly.

'Jessie's Wall,' I said, to cheer him up.

He looked at me as if he was remembering something he'd forgotten.

'Training!' he cried. 'We have to start training!'

'We're going to train Alexander,' I said quickly

to Jack. 'We agreed. Remember?'

I rushed to the fence. Alexander dropped to his feet and fled across his garden.

Alexander was always at the fence. I called him back. He came over slowly.

One of Jack's old Roman swords was lying in the flower-bed. I picked it up. It was a yellow one. It was broken. When I tried to swing it, it flopped like a trodden-on daffodil. I gave it to Alexander.

Alexander grinned at me happily.

One of Jack's old Roman helmets was lying in the flower-bed. I picked it up and plopped it on Alexander's head. 'Alexander,' I said, 'you're a Roman soldier.'

Alexander was pleased to be a Roman soldier.

'If you're a Roman soldier,' I said to him kindly, 'you have to be trained.'

Alexander nodded happily.

I led Alexander along his fence to the bottom of the garden. There were some steps on our side and a hole in the fence. Alexander put one hand on his helmet to stop it falling off and I pulled him through the hole in the fence by the other. He wouldn't let go of his sword.

'Very good, Alexander,' I said.

'Sit him on the wall,' Jack said sternly. 'First we have to find out what he knows.'

It didn't take long to find out what Alexander

knew. Alexander didn't know anything. Alexander's dad knew everything, but Alexander didn't know the alphabet, he couldn't count up to a hundred, he thought Monday came before Sunday, and he thought there were eight days in the week.

Every time Jack asked him a question, Alexander shrieked, 'Ask my dad!'

He had never heard of Augustus Caesar.

He had never even heard of the Romans.

'We're going to train you, Alexander,' I said. 'You never know, you might have a Roman temple in your garden.'

Alexander didn't know. But he sat up straight, folded his arms, and crossed his legs to listen while Jack told him all about being a Roman.

Then Jack decided to test him.

'Who used to speak Latin, Alexander?'

Alexander smiled. 'My dad?' he giggled, sitting up very straight.

'The Romans!'

'And my dad,' Alexander said.

'Was your dad a Roman?'

Alexander looked puzzled. 'What's a Roman?'

I went into the garden shed and got some spades and shovels.

'Let's train him to dig,' I said.

Jack told Alexander to stand up. 'We'll train him to do Roman marching first,' he said. 'The

Romans marched twenty miles a day with packs on their backs. Can you do that Alexander?'

Alexander nodded, smiled, giggled and hopped on one foot.

Jack pointed Alexander towards the climbing frame. 'Starting this way,' he said. 'Do seventy-three turns round the climbing frame this way, then seventy-three turns back. Then seventy-three turns this way again and seventy-three turns back.'

'He can't count,' I said.

'After that,' Jack said, 'climb the climbing frame seventy-three times. Then go round it seventy-three times. Then step up on the wall seventy-three times.'

'He won't remember,' I said.

'We'll tie a knot in his hankie.'

I looked at Alexander. His happy face was smeared with dirt and dinner, and his nose was running. Alexander's nose was always running. He was born with a running nose.

'He hasn't got a hankie,' I said. I didn't even need to ask.

'There must be something we can tie a knot in,' Jack said.

'We can tie a knot in his neck.'

'Has he got a tissue?' Jack said sternly. 'He's supposed to be a Roman soldier.'

'Let's just train him to dig.'

'He needs to march first,' Jack insisted.

I dropped the shovels and spades with a clattering noise on the patio. I went inside. I was starting to feel hungry.

Inside, the most amazing sight met my eyes.

Two smartly zipped-up suitcases stood in the passage near the front door. Beside them were several smaller bags, all packed to bursting. A neat line of wellington boots was laid out. Four bright orange anoraks were rolled into tight little bundles. And, most amazing of all, there was Big Dog sitting on the bottom step, patiently waiting, while the two Loch Ness monsters sat chattering behind him.

'We're going away!' I cried.

'We're going away!' I yelled.

'Jack!' I shrieked, running back to the garden. 'We're going! We're leaving! We're all packed up! Hurry!'

I couldn't see Alexander. Then I spotted him. He was behind the tree in his own garden. He had his helmet on, but instead of holding the daffodil-yellow sword he was holding a bucket and spade. He was digging.

5 Yorkshire Again

'I'm glad things have worked out this way,' Mum said next morning. 'I'm *so* looking forward to having a good long chat with Jessie.'

Dad grunted. He was still thinking about Hadrian's Wall.

We were all packed up and ready to set off for Yorkshire. We were waiting outside for Jack.

'Does Jessie know we're coming?' I asked.

'Of course.'

'Does she know we're coming to dig up the Roman temple and find the treasure?' That was what I really meant.

'Not exactly.' Mum looked at me very solemnly. 'All we're going to do is talk. We're going to help Jessie and Miss Fox understand each other.'

Dad grunted again. He didn't say anything, but I had the feeling he wasn't as keen on helping Jessie and Miss Fox understand each other as Mum was.

'Jessie and Miss Fox have been having a silly and unnecessary quarrel,' Mum explained grandly. 'I'm sure we can sort it out. And Patrick, I'm relying on you to be sensible.'

Sensible! I knew what being sensible meant. It meant keeping my mouth shut and my ears closed and my nose out of everything.

'You leave all the business about the temple to me,' Mum added brightly. 'Just enjoy the holiday.'

She patted me on the head.

'What *is* that boy doing?' Dad said impatiently, meaning Jack.

Mum gave herself a little shake. She tapped her foot on the pavement. 'Jack!' she cried. 'Jack! Hurry *up*. We're all waiting for you!'

She marched up the garden path. 'Hurry up, Jack,' she yelled through the front door. 'Everybody else is in the car.'

That wasn't true. We were all standing on the pavement beside the car.

'And we have a long way to go and we have to call in at the Roman Britain Living History Society on the way.'

'Oh?' said Dad, annoyed. 'Since when?'

'Since Miss Fox rang this morning.'

'Oh?' Dad didn't look pleased. 'What did she want?'

'I don't know. She didn't say.'

Standing on the pavement, Mum and Dad suddenly started having a quarrel about Miss

Fox. Dad said Miss Fox was batty. Mum said she was a kind, enthusiastic person who lived for the Romans. Dad said the Romans had been dead for two thousand years. Mum said that wasn't funny.

I said, 'If you've finished your quarrel, can we go?' I don't like it when my mum and dad quarrel.

They said, both together, 'We weren't quarrelling. We were having a conversation.'

Then they remembered Jack. 'Where is he?' Dad cried. 'Is he in the bathroom? Why does he always decide to go the minute we're ready to leave?'

'He can't help it if he needs to do a pooh!' I told my dad. 'You can't help it if you need to do a pooh.'

'Why didn't he go earlier?' Dad said. He gave me a little shove. 'Run inside and tell your brother to hurry up.'

Mum went in ahead of me. By the time I got upstairs she was outside the bathroom door, banging it, and saying, 'Come on Jack. That's enough now. You can do the rest later.'

I watched her for a bit. Then I went into the bedroom. Jack was lying on his front on the floor under the bunk beds. All I could see was his foot sticking out.

'Jack,' I said. 'We're ready to go.'

Jack sniffed.

'Are you getting your torch, Jack?' I whispered.

We would need a good torch to go digging in the middle of the night.

Jack slowly appeared. He slithered out backwards like a snake. First his legs, then his body, all covered with dust, his arms and his hands, which were empty, and his head, which was very, very, sad.

'Jack?' I said.

He looked at me sadly.

'What's the matter?'

Outside the room, I could hear Mum, thump, thump, thumping on the bathroom door. 'Come on, Jack,' she was saying. 'Pull the chain now, there's a good boy.'

'I've looked everywhere,' Jack said miserably. He stared out of big, brown, unhappy, empty eyes. 'I can't find it anywhere.'

'What?'

'*Augustus Caesar's World*,' he cried. 'It's gone. It's gone. What am I going to say to Mrs Ross?'

Jack couldn't think about anything else except what Mrs Ross would say about a boy who could lose a book about the Romans.

At last, Dad lost his patience. 'If *Augustus Caesar's World* is gone, then *Augustus Caesar's*

World is gone,' he said. 'And the sooner we forget about it, the better. Let's think about something else.'

'No!' Jack wailed.

'These things have a habit of turning up,' Dad said. 'I'm sure we'll get it back.'

'Nobody except you would want it,' I said helpfully.

'Mrs Ross wants it.' Jack said.

We got in the car and set off for Yorkshire.

'Look,' I said. I took a matchbox out of my pocket. I opened it. Inside was Nero, Jack's pet woodlouse. I was training him to like me. I was training myself to like him even when he wiggled.

Jack took Nero and slipped him in his pocket.

Suddenly, we stopped.

'Are we there?' I asked. 'That was quick.' I hadn't even had time to get hungry. Then I remembered. The Roman Britain Living History Society. We were outside it. Mum jumped out of the car.

'Don't be long,' Dad said grumpily.

'I'll only be a minute,' she said, flying up the path.

Jack quickly undid his seat-belt, opened the door on his side, and followed Mum.

Dad drummed his fingers on the steering-wheel. We waited.

'Dad,' I said, putting my arms round his neck,

'are you excited about going to Yorkshire? I am.'

He said something like, 'Humph,' and, 'Don't strangle me,' but he smiled. We started talking about Sam and Jessie.

After a bit Dad said, 'Look. There they are.' He pointed at an upstairs window.

I looked. It was them, all right: Mum and Miss Fox. They were examining some large sheets of paper, holding them up to the light and squinting.

Secret plans of the temple, of course. Maps. Probably in code. That would interest Jessie.

I hoped it wouldn't interest Jessie too much though. Mum and Miss Fox and Jessie might all gang up together and start saying things to us like, 'Don't touch, you might spoil it.' Or, 'Be careful, it's very old.'

A moment later, something like a hurricane ripped the car door open. It was Jack. He threw himself in, all arms and legs and a face that was one big exclamation mark. In his hand he was holding *Augustus Caesar's World*.

He poked it up my nose.

'Mum took it to the Roman Britain Living History Society!' he cried. 'She left it there. She forgot all about it. Miss Fox had it.'

'I told you it would turn up,' Dad said.

'She *left* it there!' Jack exclaimed. He was very angry. He started making lists of all the things

Mum had done wrong. 'First, she took my book out without asking permission. Second, she left it. Third, she forgot that she'd taken it. Fourth, she couldn't remember where she left it. Fifth . . . ' Jack searched in his mind for a fifth crime.

I felt a bit sorry for Mum. She was only trying to be helpful.

'Fifth,' Jack said, suddenly elbowing me in the ribs with the arm that wasn't poking *Augustus Caesar's World* up my nose, 'you were with her all the time. Why didn't you tell me?'

I gasped. 'Me! It wasn't my fault!'

'You were there!'

'I didn't know!'

I pushed Jack off me. Dad told us to stop quarrelling.

'Stop it,' he said, when we didn't stop. 'This is silly and unnecessary.'

'Yes,' I agreed. 'And it's not fair.'

I rubbed my nose and my ribs, folded my arms, sniffed, stuck out my bottom lip and looked out of the window.

Nobody said anything for a long time , until Jack said, 'Luckily, Miss Fox found it.'

'Miss Fox is good at finding things,' I told him. It was the only good thing I could think of just then. 'She should come to Yorkshire with us.'

I don't know what made me say it. The words just popped out.

'Oh no,' Dad suddenly cried.

At the door of the Roman Britain Living History Society were Mum and Miss Fox. Miss Fox had a tattered brown rucksack on her back. She bent down and carefully locked the door with a big key. Then she straightened up and walked by Mum's side towards the car.

'Oh no,' I said. That wasn't what I meant at all. There wasn't room in the back of our small car for Miss Fox.

I held my breath.

'She's making a bee-line for us,' Dad whispered. He seemed to be trying to shrink in his seat. 'This is taking things too far.'

But Miss Fox only came over to say hello. Then, with a cheery, 'Cheerio, see you later,' she swung off in the other direction.

Mum got into the car.

Dad said, 'That was close. For a moment I thought you'd decided to bring her with us.'

'Whatever gave you that idea?' Mum said. 'We haven't got room for Miss Fox. She's making her own way up to Yorkshire. We're going to meet her there.'

We started driving. I liked the idea of Miss Fox with her rucksack setting off for Yorkshire, but I wasn't sure what Jessie would think about it.

'Is she going to march the whole way?' I asked.

'Yes,' Dad said. 'A one-woman Roman army,

descending on the Yorkshire barbarians.'

'Don't be silly,' Mum said gaily. 'She's got a tent and a motorbike. The Romans didn't have motorbikes.'

All the way up to Yorkshire, Dad and Mum talked. At first I listened hard. I even crossed my arms and sat up straight, but bit by bit my arms slipped and my head flopped.

Jack stayed awake reading *Augustus Caesar's World*. I fell asleep reading a story about moles and badgers.

Bit by bit, when I was in the middle of having tea by the fireside with a badger, my eyes closed like a closing book. A mole hurried by. He said hello in Latin to some Roman ladies in their nightdresses. Then a tooth fairy pushed me off my chair.

I blinked.

Jack was clambering on me. 'I remember that tree!' he shouted.

'Me too!' I said.

We scrambled to the windows, seeing and blinking and remembering all at the same time.

We were driving down the lane. The lane led to another lane, the other lane led to a bridge, the bridge led to a lane, and the lane led to Jessie's house. We remembered it all.

Mum was saying, 'I wonder if Miss Fox has

arrived yet.'

Dad looked up at the sky. 'Can you see any sparks yet?'

I looked. I couldn't see any sparks.

'You will,' Dad said.

Jack screeched, 'There's Sam!'

Dad screeched to a stop.

Jessie and Sam were walking down the lane to meet us. Jessie was in a pair of overalls all spattered with paint. Her cheeks were red and shiny. Her yellow hair stuck up straight like a field of corn.

Sam loped and prowled beside her, all Sammy.

We undid our seat belts.

I screeched, 'We're here!'

Mum screeched, 'Be careful! Sit still! Wait!'

But we couldn't wait. We tumbled out of the car and fell headfirst into a lot of hugging and kissing and barking and screeching. Sam bounded up on to his hind legs. He was bigger than me. He was so excited he barked and growled and sniffed and snuffed and smothered us.

'He remembers me!' Jack cried.

'And me!' I said, as Sam's paws landed with a thud on my shoulders. My breath went.

'He missed us!' Jack exclaimed.

'Sam, Sam, Sam,' we both said, over and over

again. I was thinking, *I'll never ever leave you ever again*.

Jack picked up a stick and threw it.

'Fetch, Sam!' he yelled.

Sam flew after the flying stick. Jack scrambled after him. I scrambled after Jack. We threw, Sam fetched, we all flew. We knew our way across the fields. Better still, we knew our way to the river.

I heard Jessie cry out, 'Tea in half an hour!'

I turned to wave. Ahead of me, Jack and Sam slithered down a little dip. Across the fields, I could see Jessie's house. It was like a house in a picture, or a house in a dream.

But I couldn't see a temple. I couldn't think where a temple might be under the ground.

Jack and Sam called out to me. They were climbing over some fallen branches. They were leaping in and out of the shadows on the riverbank. They were setting up camp once more at Sam's Landing.

6 Sheep and Shocks

A strange thing happened after we arrived in Yorkshire. On the very first day, we forgot about Miss Fox. We forgot about the temple. We forgot about digging. Jack even forgot about the Romans. Well, he forgot about them a bit. *Augustus Caesar's World* lay on the window-ledge in our attic bedroom, closed.

There was lots to do. We were very busy. We had to dam the river, for one thing. We had to repair the stepping stones that led to our camp – they were much too easy to get across. We had to build a new hut for our gang in the branches of the fallen trees. And we had to start all over again teaching Sam to raise his paw and say the gang oath.

Mum and Dad started helping Jessie paint the house. It was what they always did. There was lots to do. It was taking a long time. Jessie didn't mind. 'You know what they say,' I heard her saying cheerfully to Mum. 'Rome wasn't built in a day.'

Mum gave a little gasp and buried her head in

some tins of paint stacked in a corner of the room.

Our attic bedroom was the only room that was really finished in Jessie's house. It was painted white, and there were pictures of dogs and sheep and gerbils for us to look at on the walls. Jessie was very interested in sheep. She had a poster about sheep in her bedroom, and a sticker about sheep on her van. It said: 'Little Bo-Peep had Yorkshire sheep.'

I collected some bits of sheep's wool that I found lying around in the field. I put them on the cabinet by my bed, with Tooth and King Beezy and all my best stones. There were quite a lot of things by my bed.

Everybody was very happy.

I had an extra reason for being especially happy.

My mum and dad didn't understand about not eating meat. I told them quite often that it was wicked and cruel, but it made no difference. They still ate it. But now I had someone else on my side. Jessie.

It was the first thing she told me. 'Are you still vegetarian, Patrick?' she asked.

Of course I was still vegetarian. Killing and eating living things was disgusting. I didn't know how anybody could do it.

'Good,' Jessie said. 'Because so am I.'

'Oh dear,' was all Mum could say.

Dad's face fell. He dropped his spoon into his vegetable soup. 'No more of that delicious ham?' he cried.

He looked around at the things on the table. We were having dinner. The table was crammed with delicious things. There were slices of home-made pizza, stuffed mushrooms, potato salad, cucumber, dips, pies, fruit, cream cheese, curd cheese, cottage cheese, hundreds of other cheeses and thousands of salads. Dad looked for some ham.

'Do you know what ham is?' I asked him coldly.

He looked at me. He was sad. He wanted to eat a dead pig's cooked leg.

'Would you want to eat my leg if it was cooked?' I asked him sternly.

He didn't answer.

'Pigs have feelings too,' I told him. I had to tell my parents this many times every week.

Jessie understood more than Mum and Dad about being kind to animals and wanting to look after them. But even Jessie could be wicked and cruel. That evening she gave us a terrible shock.

It was bedtime. Jessie was putting us to bed. We were very, very tired.

She tucked us in. 'Are you snug as bugs in rugs?'

59

Yes, we were snug as bugs in rugs.

'Shall I read you a story?' she asked.

We were too tired for a story.

'A poem?'

We didn't feel like a poem.

'A nursery rhyme?'

We were too old for nursery rhymes. Jessie didn't believe us.

'I know. I'll sing you 'Mary had a little lamb', she said.

Jack groaned.

'No,' I said. 'You can't.'

'I won't listen,' Jack said. He put his head under the covers.

But Jessie was already singing. She sang very sweetly.

'Mary had a little lamb
She tied it to a pylon
A thousand volts whizzed through its tum
And turned its wool to nylon!'

'Jessie!' I cried, suddenly waking up. I was suddenly wide, wide awake. I sat up in bed angrily. 'That's horrible!'

'Jessie!' said Jack, throwing his quilt off and sitting bolt upright in bed. 'That's mean! That's horrible! How could you? Poor little lamb.'

Jessie laughed so much she fell over.

'Jessie, that was a horrid thing to sing,' I told

her. 'It's not funny. It's cruel, and wicked, and horrid. Now we won't be able to get to sleep and it'll be all your fault.'

'Yes,' said Jack. 'You should never tell children horrible things just before they go to sleep. Don't you know anything? We might have night-mares.'

'You'd better tell us something nice,' I said firmly. 'Go on.' I folded my arms, closed my eyes, and waited.

There was a little pause while Jessie thought.

'I don't know anything nice.'

'You must know something.'

'Little Bo-Peep has lost her sheep?'

'No!' Jack said. 'Nothing about sheep. We've had enough about sheep. I don't trust you.'

Jessie thought harder. 'Rock-a-bye-baby in the treetops, When the wind blows the cradle will rock . . . ?'

'No!' I said. 'Stop! That's too sad.'

'It's just a nursery rhyme.'

'Well, it's not very cheerful, is it?' Jack exclaimed. 'Some idiot sticks a baby at the top of a tree on a weak branch just before a storm. The wind blows, the branch breaks and the baby crashes to the ground. Very nice.'

I'd never thought of it like that before. But Jack was right. Poor baby.

Jessie hummed and ummed and ermed, trying

to think of something nice. 'Humpty-Dumpty sat on a wall, Humpty-Dumpty had a great fall . . . ?'

'No!' I said.

'But he's only an egg!'

'No. He gets smashed all to pieces!'

'Jack and Jill went up the . . . ?'

'No!' said Jack at once.

'Little Miss Muffett sat on a . . . '

'No!' I said.

'Why not? Miss Muffett only has a little fright. Nothing horrible happens to her.'

'What about the spider?'

Jessie stared at me, puzzled.

'Didn't something horrible happen to the spider? It had a horrible fright,' I said.

'Yes,' said Jack. 'The poor spider was more frightened than that silly Miss Muffett on her tuffet spilling curds and whey all over everywhere. Anyway, what is curds and whey?'

'What's a tuffet?'

'I don't know!' Jessie roared, flinging her arms wide. 'I only wanted to tell you a bedtime story.'

Mum put her head round the door. 'Everybody settled?' she said happily. 'Snug as bugs in rugs? Happy and tired out? Isn't the air wonderful up here? Hasn't Jessie made a lovely job of the attic?' She stopped. 'Is something wrong?'

Jessie's bottom lip was sticking out and her

sticking up yellow hair was sticking up straighter than ever. Jack was saying, very grumpily, 'Well you *should* know what curds and whey are. This is the country, isn't it?'

Mum said, 'I hope the boys aren't being any trouble.'

Dad appeared in the doorway behind Mum. 'Do you know what the time is?' he said. 'Are you boys going to settle down? It's half past nine.'

They wanted us to settle down and go to sleep so that they could settle down to a big feast downstairs. I could smell it. It smelled delicious, warm and oozy and tomatoey.

I could feel an empty tummy brewing.

It wasn't fair.

'I can't sleep.' I said. 'I'm too hungry.'

'Nonsense. You're just over-excited.'

Mum tried to tuck me into bed, but I did a somersault and dived headfirst under the bed-clothes.

I bounced up and down on my hands and knees. I could hear Dad saying, 'Half past nine already. They really ought to settle down now.'

I suddenly remembered a rhyme the girls in my Saturday-morning acting class sang. I didn't like the girls in my acting class. They laughed at my cart-wheels. But if you're going to be an actor, like me, you mustn't mind if people laugh at you.

So I threw off the covers and stood up on the bed and started singing:

> 'What's the time?
> Ten to nine
> Hang your knickers
> On the line
> When they're dry
> Bring them in
> Put them in
> The biscuit tin
> Eat a biscuit
> Eat a cake
> Eat your knickers
> By mistake!'

'Yuk,' Jack said. 'That's disgusting.'

Jessie started laughing.

Mum and Dad both said, 'That's quite enough now. Get into bed and go to sleep.'

'What shall I do if I can't sleep?'

'You will,' Mum said.

'Count sheep.' Dad said.

'Can't sleep, count sheep,' Jack chanted. He started bouncing on his bed, too.

'No!' I wailed. 'I can't count sheep! Not now!'

Jessie knew what I meant.

'Jessie,' Mum said. 'Perhaps it's better if you go downstairs. I'll deal with Patrick. He's over-excited.'

The last bit, about me being over-excited, was said in a whisper. A very loud whisper. The sort of whisper actors whisper when they're whispering in a play.

'She's cruel to lambs,' I said, pointing at Jessie. 'And sheep. And spiders. And babies in cradles. And eggs.'

'And curds and whey,' Jack said. 'Did you know,' he said, 'in the old days, eating live spiders used to be a cure for the plague? They put butter on them first. To help them slide down.'

'Yuk,' I said. 'Poor spiders.'

7   No Foraging, Some Finding

Jack didn't forget about the Romans for long.

On the second morning I opened my eyes and saw Sam. He was frowning. Jack was showing him a picture in *Augustus Caesar's World*.

'Wake up,' Jack said to me. 'Get up. It's late.'

I looked at my watch. It wasn't very late. It was half past five.

The sun was shining like a bright gold coin.

'Come on,' Jack said. He pulled his socks and shoes on. 'Hurry up.'

I got up slowly, patted Sam slowly, and started slowly getting dressed.

'Come on,' Jack said.

I yawned. So did Sam.

'I'll get the shovels and spades out of the shed.'

Jack picked up *Augustus Caesar's World*. Before I could stop him, he cried, 'Come on, Sam!' and disappeared out of the door.

'Wait!' I cried. 'You've forgotten something.'

Jack came back.

'We can't start digging yet,' I said, remembering something about the Romans. 'We have to do some foraging first.'

I hurried into my clothes and we raced down the stairs, keeping a good lookout for Jessie on the way.

We got to the kitchen without seeing her. We stood there, panting a bit, listening. Everything was still. All the chairs and tables and cupboards and kettles and pots and pans were sitting in their places, just waiting, thinking.

The door to the cold-store was closed.

We opened it.

The cold-store, where Jessie kept all the food, was as big as a small room. And like a room, you had to walk into it. We liked to walk into it quite often. In the middle there was a wooden table. On the table there were always some interesting things, like cheese-and-tomato pizzas and the bits of apple pies that everybody was too full to eat.

Jack held Sam.

Sam liked foraging. He was interested in things like pizzas and pies, crisps and biscuits, honey sandwiches, bananas, buns. He was interested in meat, too, but we didn't give him any.

The store-room smelled of apples, lemons, and honey. It was dark and dusty, but shiny too, with sparkling pots of jam and lemon curd all twinkling in the gloom like fairy lights on a Christmas tree.

We nosed our way in.

But something was wrong. Something strange was sticking up out of something on the table. We went closer.

'What is it?' I whispered.

I could see a loaf of bread, a dagger stuck into it, and a piece of paper.

Before I could stop myself, I blurted, 'Is it about buried treasure? Is it a map telling us where to find the treasure?'

'Hush,' Jack whispered.

'Is it in code?'

We leaned across the table.

Jack pulled the dagger out of the bread. He eased the paper off the blade of the dagger. There wasn't any blood on it. He smoothed the paper out. It was old, crinkly, yellowy. It looked as if it had been there for hundreds of years.

'It's too dark,' Jack said. 'We need a light. Have you got a candle?'

I didn't have a candle.

'Perhaps it's in invisible writing,' I said. 'We'll have to hold it up to a fire to read it. And then work out the code.' I was good at working out codes. I hoped it was in code.

Jack screwed up his eyes. But it wasn't really

too dark. Jack wanted it to be dark. And anyway, there was an electric light in the cold-store. I went over and turned it on.

'Let me see,' I hissed, snatching the paper from Jack while he was protesting about the light.

Something looked familiar.

I pushed Jack to one side and kept him there with my elbows while I had a good look at the piece of paper. Someone had drawn some pictures all around the edges.

'Sheep,' I told Jack. 'Little, grey, woolly sheep.'

I kept my elbows out to stop him pushing me off. There was something else. Two words were written, very faintly, in the middle of the page.

I read them.

'Give it to me,' Jack insisted. 'Does it say anything?'

'It's a message from Jessie,' I told him sadly. 'It says, NO FORAGING.'

'No foraging?' Jack exclaimed in astonishment. 'Show me that.'

He snatched the paper from me.

'What does it mean?' he said.

Jack knew what 'foraging' meant. He knew what 'no' meant.

'It means Jessie's in charge up here,' I said. Jack knew that. He couldn't have forgotten that.

Jessie was strict about certain things. 'And it means she's remembering about the Romans.'

'But how did she know?' Jack gasped.

'What?'

'About foraging!' Jack stared at me out of two round scary eyes.

A shiver went through me.

'How did she know we were going to go foraging this morning?'

I shook my head. My teeth started rattling without warning. They sounded very loud in the quiet early-morning darkness of the cold-store.

'Someone must have told her,' Jack said. 'You must have told her.'

'I didn't!'

'You must have said something about the Romans.'

'I didn't!'

'You must have,' said Jack.

'I didn't! I didn't!' I cried.

Jack's eyes narrowed. 'What about when you were talking about climbing yesterday? What about when you were talking about her wall?'

'No!' I said.

But then I remembered something. It wasn't about the Romans, exactly.

'Well?' Jack said.

'I didn't say anything about the Romans,' I told Jack. 'All I said was that her wall was nicer

than Hadrian's Wall. That's not saying anything about the Romans! And I wasn't talking about foraging. I was talking about climbing!'

Jack didn't understand about climbing. He wasn't very interested in Jessie's Wall.

'We didn't talk about the Romans,' I said. 'You don't talk about the Romans when you're talking about climbing. You talk about climbing.'

Jack didn't say anything.

'At least,' I said, thinking about it a bit more, '*I* don't talk about the Romans and nor does Jessie. *You* might.'

Sam barked.

'Hush, Sam,' Jack said. He wasn't paying any attention to me now. He was staring at the piece of paper once more. He was repeating in a steady, puzzled voice, 'No foraging. No foraging.'

'If Miss Fox talked about climbing, she might talk about the Romans,' I said. 'I suppose.'

Remembering the Romans reminded me of Miss Fox. But I was sure I didn't say anything to Jessie about the Romans. I wouldn't dare. I noticed Mum and Dad didn't dare, either.

There was a sudden roaring from somewhere in the house. Sam leapt, barking. I dived under the table.

'Quick!' Jack cried. 'Let's get out of here!'

The roaring was coming nearer. It was Jessie.

Jack grabbed hold of my collar and yanked me out from under the table. We tore the door open. It was a pity to leave empty-handed, but a sound like thunder was coming towards us. Sam's four feet left the ground as we all tumbled in a flurry of arms and legs out of the cold-store, out of the kitchen, into the garden and towards the steep field.

At the top of the steep field a slope rolled down to the river where it bent in a giant U-shape to go round Jessie's house.

We ran, with Sam at our heels, till we reached the top of the field. Then we caught our breath. We sat in the long grass, breathing and waiting for something to happen. Nothing happened.

We rolled down the slope a few times, seeing who could get furthest. Then we tried rolling up. We waited for something to happen.

'Jack,' I said. 'I'm hungry.'

Jack was lying with his face in the grass. 'Did you know,' he said, 'an acre of grassland can hold more than three million earthworms?'

'What's an acre?'

'And two million spiders. Look.'

I looked. At first I couldn't see anything. Then I saw what Jack could see. It was a huge spider's web hanging between two blades of grass.

'And here,' Jack said, getting to his feet. 'And here.'

They were everywhere. The whole field was full of wispy spider's webs.

'Just think,' said Jack. 'These spiders making these webs are the great-great-great-great-great-great-grandchildren of those spiders who got spread with butter and swallowed.'

'How do you know?' I said. But I wasn't very interested. I was interested in other things spread with butter. Toast, for instance. Crumpets. Muffins.

'And if you ever see a cockroach,' Jack went on, 'don't kill it. It has Roman ancestry. Caesar might have stepped on its brother.'

'Oh, dear,' I said, padding behind Jack.

All the while we were talking we had been crossing the field, pointing out spider's webs to each other as we went.

Now we found ourselves at a drystone wall.

Sam scrambled over.

'Come on,' Jack said, quickly following Sam.

'I'm hungry!' I wailed. I wanted to go back, but I didn't want to go on my own, and, besides, I liked climbing walls.

I lunged forward and pulled myself up. Two big flat stones, balanced on top of the wall, clattered wildly. Some small stones fell behind me. The wall was loose.

I had to jump.

But there was no time. The stones began to shift and slip.

My stomach swooped up into my mouth and stayed there. I put out a foot to steady myself. The stone slid. I put out a hand to steady myself. The stone under my hand slid. I slid. The whole wall slid.

I slipped and slid.

All the stones began sliding out of the wall. They made a sort of grinding, clacking noise behind me. They were tumbling and tinkling like teeth out of a giant's mouth. And I was in the middle of them. I was getting mashed.

'Help!' I cried.

The round hard stones rolled me in a slithering, slipping, sliding heap to the ground.

Would they roll me underground? Would I fall down a long dark tunnel where moles and badgers lived? Would I drink a drink that shrunk me?

I came to a stop. I uncovered my face and looked.

Jack and Sam were staring at me with their mouths open.

'I'm all right!' I said bravely.

Later I would count my scratches and bruises. I hoped there would be lots.

'You're all right,' Jack said, in a startled voice.

'But look what's happened to the wall.'

I looked behind me.

There wasn't any wall. Not behind me. Behind me was a flat pile of stones. It was like the high part of a very pebbly beach, where the pebbles are big and never get wet by the sea.

'Jessie will kill you,' Jack told me.

'It wasn't my fault!'

'Jessie will still kill you.'

Jack walked away.

'Come back!' I cried, scratching my leg on something as I struggled to my feet. 'Help me put it back!'

'How?'

I looked at what used to be a wall. Perhaps I wasn't all right after all. Perhaps I needed to go to hospital.

I sat down. My legs were trembling. I felt very not all right.

Perhaps later we could put the wall back together again. Perhaps Mum and Dad would help.

Miserably, sitting in the ruins of the wall, I picked up a stone and balanced it on top of another one. It didn't look right. It wobbled.

I tried some other stones. I put medium-sized stones on top of big ones, and little stones on top of medium-sized stones. I didn't do it very well. It was hard work.

I spotted a really huge, square-shaped stone. It was a strange stone, different to the others. It was nice and flat, but with round marks and squiggles all over it. I pulled at it by one corner. I couldn't shift it. I pulled by another corner. It was no use.

'What's that?' Jack had come back. He stood with his feet firmly planted on a pile of stones and he pointed.

I looked.

Under the stone, I saw something that was the colour of dusty honey. It was a piece of pot. It was jagged at the edges and cracked.

I crawled over and picked it up.

'It's Roman!' Jack said excitedly. Before I could stop him, he snatched it from me. 'Look!' he said, holding the pot far away from me so that I couldn't look. 'These are Roman markings!'

'Show me.'

Painfully, I got to my feet. It was hard trying to balance on the mixed up mess of big stones and little stones. It was even harder trying to catch Jack. Every time I came up close to look, he skipped away.

'It is Roman!' he exclaimed. 'It is! It is!'

'How do you know?'

'I know,' he said. He put his hand on the back of his neck. 'The hairs on my neck are prickling. That's how you can tell.'

'Really?'

Jack nodded.

'And,' he said, 'an ice-cold shiver ran down my back the moment I spotted it. I knew.'

I stared at Jack, open-mouthed.

'And,' he said, 'there's a picture of a pot just like this in *Augustus Caesar's World*.

8   Quite a Few Mistakes

Jack found it, but I picked it up first. After a long argument, we agreed that it belonged to both of us.

It was our first Roman find. We called it Pot o'the Wall. Jack chose the name.

Carefully, we took Pot o'the Wall up to our attic bedroom. We went the back way. We crept quietly. A storm was roaring round inside the house. There were great booming explosions of thunder. Lightning ripped. Sparks flew.

It was Jessie.

'Mum must have said something to Jessie,' Jack said. 'I wonder what she said.'

We settled Pot o'the Wall down with Big Dog and King Beezy and the Loch Ness monsters.

The attic door opened quietly and Mum crept in.

'Patrick,' she said. 'Jack. Did one of you boys by any chance say anything to Jessie about . . . you know . . . the Romans?'

'Patrick did,' Jack said at once.

'I didn't.'

'Oh, dear,' Mum said. 'Someone did.'

'Well, it wasn't me,' I said. 'Look what I found.' I showed her Pot o'the Wall. 'It's Roman. Feel how rough and old it feels.'

Mum took our Roman piece of pottery. She turned it over once or twice in her hand, but without really looking. 'Very nice,' she said, glancing nervously over her shoulder.

'It's a Roman cup,' I said. 'A pot. Like all those pots Miss Fox has got.'

Mum smiled. She handed Pot o'the Wall back to me, saying, 'That would be nice, but it isn't very likely is it?'

The attic door opened quietly and Dad crept in.

'Did somebody say something to Jessie?' he whispered.

'Patrick did,' Mum said.

'I didn't,' I cried.

'Oh, dear,' Dad said. 'That was a mistake.'

We all sat on my bed. Mum explained that Jessie got upset when people mentioned the Romans.

'Why?' Jack scowled.

Dad explained that Jessie was interested in the people who lived in Yorkshire before the Romans came.

'The barbarians?' I said brightly. I was pleased I remembered.

'Sshhh,' Mum said, shivering.

'Don't use that word,' said Dad.

'Why not?'

'You see, boys,' Dad began. 'It's like this.' He took a deep breath. 'The Romans called everyone who wasn't Roman a barbarian. And because the Romans were very civilized and good at doing things . . . '

'The Romans were good at everything,' Jack said.

'They built straight roads,' I said. I remembered quite a lot.

Mum smiled at me. 'Let Daddy explain,' she said.

Dad thought hard. 'Perhaps you'd better tell them,' he said to Mum.

'It's quite simple,' Mum said. 'Jessie gets very upset when people call the people who lived in Yorkshire before the Romans came barbarians. To say someone is a barbarian is to say they're wild, rough, noisy, fierce . . . '

'Like Jessie?' I said. Jessie could be quite fierce. She could be quite noisy too.

'Patrick!' Mum and Dad both cried.

'I fell off a wall,' I said quickly. They were both glaring at me wildly, fiercely.

It worked. Mum and Dad suddenly looked very, very worried.

'Look.' I showed them my arms and legs. I had

to show them. They never notice anything! Luckily, my arms and legs were a sorry sight. They were scraped and scratched, grazed and scabbed, pricked and bruised. And they were dirty.

'Goodness gracious!' Mum said.

Dad took me to the bathroom to wash my cuts. 'Unless you'd rather lick your wounds?' he said.

Yuk.

He stood me on a stool by the bathroom window.

'This will sting a bit,' he said, pouring something out of a bottle into the warm water in the sink. 'Wait a minute.'

He disappeared. A moment later he came back.

'Bite on this.' He held out an orange. 'And it's probably better if you don't look. Look out of the window and think about something else.'

Dad dipped a wad of cotton wool in the water and started stabbing my legs. It hurt. I bit on the orange and looked as hard as I could out of the window.

At first all I saw was the garden, the woods, the steep field and all the long lines of purple hills in the distance. Then I saw something else. It was certainly something else to think about.

'Keep still, ' Dad said. 'You've been very brave so far.'

I nearly said something, but my mouth was stuffed with orange. My teeth were sinking into orange. Orangey spit was dribbling all round.

I closed my eyes and opened them again. Perhaps I imagined what I saw. No. It was still there. It was quite a long way away. Not as far as the purple hills but not as near as the steep field. In between the two.

It was a tent. Beside the tent was a motorbike. Someone was moving slowly round the tent, banging in tent pegs.

Once again, with a horrible lurching, up swooped my insides. Over went my stomach. The orange burst from my lips as if something inside had punched it. I choked and caught my breath.

'Steady on,' Dad said. 'Almost finished.'

The thunderstorm was raging inside the house.

'Dad?' I said. My eyes were fixed on the figure moving round the tent. 'When is Mum going to tell Jessie that Miss Fox is in Yorkshire?'

Dad shuddered.

'What will Jessie say when she tells her?'

'Quite a lot, I expect. Patrick,' he said suddenly, 'how good are you at tongue twisters?'

'What's a tongue twister?'

'Peggy Babcock.'

'Who's she?'

'Who's who?' my dad said, as if he didn't know what I was talking about. He poured some more out of the bottle into the sink. He took a huge wad of cotton wool.

'Who's Peggy Babcock?' I said. 'Peggy Bag-cock. Beggy Bagcop. Keppy Bagpop. Ow!'

'Finished,' Dad announced.

Miss Simms, my teacher, says that when you make a big mistake it doesn't matter, as long as you know you've made a mistake. She says we learn by making mistakes.

My mum made a big mistake about Jessie and the Roman temple.

For one thing, it was a big mistake even to mention the word 'Romans' near Jessie.

Jessie's storm lasted the whole day. We stayed down by the river where everything was quiet and calm.

Next morning, before we went down to break-fast, Mum said, 'Whatever you do, don't men-tion Miss Fox. Jessie doesn't know about Miss Fox, yet.'

'Nasty, horrible people,' Jessie said at once, meaning the Romans. 'Marching through other people's countries! March, march, march. Stealing other people's countries! Swipe, swipe, swipe. Looting. Pillaging. Burning.'

'What's looting?' I said. 'What's pillaging?'

'Hush,' Mum said. 'Eat your breakfast.'

'Stealing,' said Jessie, looking at me as if she was glad I'd asked. 'Destroying. Doing not very nice things to the nice Yorkshire people who were here already.'

'The Romans . . . ' Mum said.

'The Romans!' Jessie roared. A great shower of toast exploded from her lips. Smoke steamed from the top of her head. 'The Romans! I never want to hear the word Roman again as long as I live.'

'Crumbs!' Jack cried.

The table was covered with them.

'I don't see what's so bad about the Romans,' Mum said, making another mistake.

'Romans, Romans, Romans!' cried Jessie. 'Romans this. Romans that. Romans here. Romans there. Romans in your underwear! I'm sick of the Romans!'

Mum sniffed. She looked hurt. She bit a corner of toast and honey in a hurt sort of way.

How did Jessie know about the Roman man in his underwear? Did Jessie have a cardboard picture with clothes with tabs on them to colour and cut out?

'What's so special about the Romans?' said Jessie, flinging herself on a little raisin cake and drowning it in yoghurt.

That looked a good idea. I did the same.

I dripped a drip of honey on top. It tasted good.

Very patiently, Mum started to tell Jessie what was special about the Romans. She told her about straight roads and hot baths and Hadrian's Wall.

Jack told her about centurions, gladiators and charioteers.

Jessie put her fingers in her ears.

Without taking her fingers out of her ears, Jessie explained to me about the people who lived a long, long, long time before the Romans came to Yorkshire. They were much nicer than the Romans. She was interested in them.

She said she would tell me about them if I was interested.

I said 'yes' because that was the polite thing to say. I thought they sounded quite boring.

But they were nice to their animals. The Romans were not very nice to their animals. The Romans were horrible to their lions. They made them eat people.

'There were people here, in Yorkshire, before the Romans came marching and swiping and stealing,' Jessie said to me. 'They made interesting carvings on stones. The stones are out there on the moors. It's easy enough to find them. But nobody knows what they mean.'

'That's interesting,' I said, dripping a bit more

honey on my yoghurt, on my raisin cake, on my plate, on the table.

'These stones are only found in Yorkshire,' Jessie went on. 'They're called cup and ring stones.'

'That's a funny name for a stone,' I said. Honey was dripping down my arm. I licked it. It tasted of scratches. My arm was covered in scratches.

'You can see a shape like the bottom of a cup.' Jessie picked up a cup and showed me. 'And there's a ring round it. Cup and ring. It's easy.'

'What were they for?'

'Nobody knows what the stones were for.' Jessie's fingers went back in her ears, but she seemed to be able to hear whatever she wanted to hear. 'They might have had something to do with magic. Or battle. Or worship. Or they could even be strange sorts of stone maps, lying on the moors, telling people which way to go. Nobody knows.'

She took her fingers out of her ears and drew a picture of a cup and ring stone. It looked like one of Jessie's letters, all squiggles and funny writing with little drawings round the edges. In the middle, she drew lots of cup shapes with rings round them.

Mum said, 'Patrick will enjoy colouring that in, later.'

Dad said, 'He can cut it out and make a model.'

Dad was very keen on models.

'This cup and ring stone,' Jack began. He looked at the picture suspiciously. 'Someone must know what it was for.'

'Nobody knows,' Jessie said. She smiled. 'It's quite nice that nobody knows, don't you think?'

Jack didn't think it was nice that nobody knew. Nor did I. I was sure that we would know what the stones were for if we found one.

'And there are standing stones,' said Jessie. 'Ancient stones, far older than the Romans. Tossed by giants.'

'Giants?' Jack and I both said.

'Who knows?' said Jessie. 'Nobody knows. This land is riddled with mystery.'

'And under the land,' Mum said eagerly. 'There's mystery under the ground, too. Mystery just waiting to be discovered.'

'Like temples!' I cried.

I remembered the picture Miss Fox showed me.

'Temples made out of gold bricks,' I said. 'Tossed by Romans.'

Jack laughed. He started telling Jessie about the Temple of the Vestals, in Rome, where young priestesses guarded a sacred flame that was never allowed to go out. But Jessie didn't want to know about Jack's temple. She wanted to know about mine.

'Gold bricks?' she looked at me, puzzled. I felt very happy all of a sudden, thinking about the temple in the picture Miss Fox showed me. The temple under Jessie's garden.

Everything was going to end happily. Jessie would like to hear about the temple, and she would like to dig it up and we would like to help her. Sam would help too. He was good at digging. He didn't need to be trained. We would do it very carefully, so that we didn't scratch the beautiful gold dome. We would tell Sam to be careful. And when we'd finished, there would be a beautiful white and gold temple standing and shining brightly in Jessie's garden.

'Your temple,' I said. 'Under your garden.' I nudged her cheerily with my elbow.

Jack didn't like it when I talked about the Romans. He started making funny noises and jiggling at Jessie's other arm.

'Under my garden?' Jessie said.

Jack bounced out of his chair. 'Take no notice of him. He's bonkers,' he cried. 'But there may have been a temple. It's true. It's possible!'

'A lovely white and gold temple,' I said happily. 'And blue sky and ladies in white and gold nightdresses.' How could I have forgotten?

Jessie stared and stared. 'Under the ground? Here? At Ugglemarsby?'

'Yes,' I said excitedly.

'No!' Jack groaned. 'Not white and gold night-dresses!'

'Blue sky? Under the ground? Patrick,' Jessie said, 'I don't know what it's like where you live, but we don't have that sort of thing in Yorkshire. We like to have our blue sky over our heads, not under our feet.'

She put her hand on my forehead. 'Are you feeling all right?' she asked. 'Have you got a temperature?'

'It's true!'

'He's bonkers,' Jack said.

Mum said, 'Patrick may have got the wrong end of the stick.'

'What stick?' I cried.

'But, Jessie,' Mum said urgently, 'if Miss Fox has her facts straight, there's an exciting discovery to be made here. I think she told you in her letter. The site of a temple. Post holes and trenches, and perhaps some other interesting things besides.'

There was a silence. Everybody seemed to be waiting for somebody else to speak.

Jessie said, 'Did you say Miss Fox?'

'I was going to tell you!' Mum exclaimed. 'I've been meaning to tell you. Such an extraordinary coincidence! You'll never guess!'

All in a rush, Mum began telling Jessie about Hadrian's Wall, and planning a Roman holiday, and being sorry Hadrian's Wall wasn't in Yorkshire, and going to see Miss Fox. Jack began telling her about the Romans marching in straight lines the length and breadth of the country, leaving broken pots behind them as they went. We all tried to explain about the temple. Jessie held up her hands and begged us to speak one at a time, but she soon gave that up. Our words tumbled out. We told her everything, everything Miss Fox said, everything we said, everything we expected her to say. Once we started, we couldn't stop.

'And even if you aren't interested in the Romans,' I said breathlessly, 'you must be interested in this. There's a picture of your temple. Miss Fox showed me a picture.'

Jessie asked me very kindly what sort of a picture Miss Fox showed me.

I told her.

Jack hooted and howled behind me.

'I see,' Jessie said. She didn't say anything else.

Mum said, 'Nobody said gold bricks exactly. Nobody meant a temple exactly. Not standing exactly.'

Didn't they?

'Not exactly,' Mum said.

'Miss Fox said!' I said. 'She showed me a picture!'

Mum wriggled uncomfortably. 'It wasn't exactly a picture of Jessie's temple.'

'Yes, it was.'

'No, it wasn't,' Mum said impatiently. 'It was a picture of a temple like the temple that might have stood here in Roman times.'

'No!'

'Perhaps it was a photograph,' Jack said in a baby voice, hooting horribly and laughing. 'Perhaps they had photographs in Roman times.'

Jessie said, 'Patrick, I think it's time *I* showed you a picture.'

Before Jack could stop her, Jessie whipped *Augustus Caesar's World* out from under him, and started turning the pages until she came to the picture she wanted.

'Look, Patrick,' she said, holding it out to me. 'This is what archaeologists mean when they talk about finding a temple.'

I put my hands over my eyes. I wasn't sure I wanted to look. Looking at people's pictures had caused me quite a lot of trouble already.

'Go on,' Jessie said. 'It won't bite.'

I took my hands away and looked. I saw a small coloured picture of the ground. I looked closer. I could see a few holes in the ground. It wasn't a very interesting picture.

'What does it say underneath?' Jessie murmured.

It said a lot underneath. 'Ah, yes,' Jessie said, reading it out loud over my shoulder. 'Frightfully exciting discovery, blah blah. Stunningly well-preserved example, blah blah. Super-duper site blah.'

'What is it?'

'Layers and layers of earth.'

'I tried to tell him,' Jack said.

There was nothing there. No high white pillars. No gold bricks. No lovely gold dome. No ladies holding up trays of candles.

Mum said, 'Not exactly nothing. There are some holes in the ground. The holes are very important. Very interesting. A hole in the ground can be very interesting.'

A hole in the ground. Not a temple. A hole in the ground. Not treasure.

I looked at all the faces round me. I was very, very disappointed. I was especially disappointed in Jack. He knew about the Romans. He said it was a temple. He didn't say it was a hole in the ground.

I said to Jessie, 'But where is the temple?'

'Where are the Romans?' Jessie said. She snapped her fingers. She blew a puff of wind. 'Gone. The wind blew them away. Puff.'

Later, when we were clearing the table, Jessie whispered in my ear. 'But I'm glad about one thing about the Romans.'

'What?'

'The Romans brought you back here. Perhaps this time your parents will decide to stay.'

Later still she said, 'Welcome back to Yorkshire, Patrick.' Forget about digging. We have some climbing to do.'

9   The Magpie

The sun was shining. In Yorkshire it rains a lot. Jessie wanted it to rain.

'It'll rain soon,' Dad said gloomily, looking out of a window. Everything sparkled in the sunlight.

'Bound to rain soon,' Mum said. 'Sunshine like this can't last.'

'We'd better get a move on then,' said Jessie. 'If we're going to get any serious climbing in.'

She was sorting out the climbing and abseiling gear. It was all dumped in a mangled heap in the back garden by the climbing wall.

Mum and Dad and Jack all suddenly discovered some important things they had to do. Dad had to clean a bit of mud off his boots, Mum had to sort out the old newspapers, and Jack had to sit with Sam.

I was the only person who was interested in climbing and abseiling. I was very interested.

The gear was very interesting. Jessie pulled things out, one by one, and handed them to me.

We checked the abseiling gear first.

'This is a crab,' she said.

She showed me how it worked.

'This is a sit harness. For abseiling. Let's try it on.'

She held up something that looked like yellow bandages.

I had to step into one end of the sit harness. The other end went over my shoulders. Then Jessie grabbed hold of the bottom end and grabbed hold of the top end and yanked the two together.

I doubled over, yowling.

'Good,' Jessie said.

She hooked the crab into both parts of the harness and tied me up like a parcel. Then she looped a long red rope through the crab.

Still holding the rope, Jessie stepped into the heap of gear and picked out a helmet. She put it on my head.

'Good,' she said. 'Let's test it.'

It was hard to walk in the sit harness, but Jessie wanted to try out the gear on a tree with a low branch before we went up the wall.

She swung the rope over. She tied support ropes and tested them.

'Are you sure the branch is strong enough?' I said.

Jessie was sure. She hooked me to the support ropes.

'Safe as a baby,' she cried, as she gave a gigantic tug on the red rope. The ground left my feet. I found myself floating bumpily up, my arms and legs dangling, up, up into the leafy tree.

'What does it feel like?' Jessie called out.

It felt like being a crab. Or an octopus. Or a spider. Something with lots of bits dangling. It felt like being a bird, snug in a nest high in the trees. It felt like being on a mattress made of air. It felt very nice.

The wind swung me lazily round.

It swung me the other way. I closed my eyes.

Slowly, Jessie brought me down to the ground. I landed with a very small bump.

I couldn't understand why Mum and Dad and Jack didn't want to have a go. It was wonderful.

'Hands here. Feet there,' Jessie said. 'Let's see what you remember.'

We were on the climbing wall. We were trying a new way up to the top. It was harder than the old way, but it was still easy. I had to spread myself like a starfish. Most important of all, I had to make sure I didn't look down.

'Look sideways,' Jessie said.

I looked sideways. My heart swooped up into my mouth.

I'd forgotten about Miss Fox.

There was her tent. There was her motorbike, propped up beside the tent. But where was Miss Fox?

We went up the wall slowly and carefully. Jessie climbed beside me. I was learning the right way to climb, hands here, feet there, exactly as Jessie told me. I breathed brick. I tried not to look at the tent. I tried not to think about Miss Fox.

There was another thing I was trying not to think about, too. The other wall. The broken wall. What would Jessie say when she found out? From the top of Jessie's roof, you could see everything. When we got to the roof, would she see the wall? What would I say? What would Jessie say?

We climbed, slowly and carefully.

Jessie said, 'Have you remembered the two golden rules about climbing?'

'Don't look down,' I said, not looking down. 'And only think about climbing.'

'Good,' Jessie said.

Halfway up, there was a new resting place. It was a covered ledge that went a little way into the wall, like a tunnel. We crouched inside, resting.

We munched apples from the cold store.

'Jessie,' I said, remembering something. 'How did you know about foraging?'

Jessie laughed. 'A little bird whispered in my ear.'

She started getting to her feet. I was happy

climbing with Jessie. If only I could have stopped myself thinking things I didn't want to think about. But you can't stop yourself thinking, even when you don't want to.

'Just a minute,' Jessie said. Something bright and shiny was glittering in the dust right where we were sitting.

Jessie reached behind me and picked it up. It was a little shiny object, quite small and oddly shaped. It was gold. A jewel.

'Treasure!' I started to say.

But even before the word was out, I remembered there wasn't a temple. There wasn't any treasure.

Jessie showed it to me. We both peered at it.

'It's a bunch of grapes,' said Jessie, turning the little object round and round. 'Look. Here's the stalk. And these are the grapes. And these are leaves.' She pointed, one by one, to the different bits. She sounded very puzzled.

'It's not treasure,' I said. 'Don't think it's a bit of buried treasure.'

'I don't think it's buried treasure,' Jessie exclaimed. 'Who would bury treasure up here?'

We were quite a long way away from the ground.

'It *isn't* buried treasure,' I told her.

I had an idea what it was. I was bursting to say.

'What can it be?' Jessie murmured and muttered.

'I know what it is,' I said proudly.

'What?'

'It's stolen jewellery. And I know who stole it!'

'Who?'

I knew. I pointed to the tree with the low branch. 'See that nest?'

Jessie peered. There were lots of nests in the tree. In fact, there were quite a lot of trees just there at the edge of the field. In fact, the edge of the field was the edge of the little wood so it was all trees.

'What nest?' Jessie said in a grumpy sort of way. 'Which tree?'

'Any tree!' I said. 'Think! Magpies!'

Jessie looked at the jewel and looked at the tree.

'Magpies love stealing jewellery,' I told her. 'They pick it up in their beaks and take it to their nests.'

'But this isn't a magpie's nest.'

That was true. 'But the magpie might have *thought* it was a nest.'

'Why?'

'I don't know. Perhaps it couldn't see very well.'

'No.' Jessie shook her head.

'Perhaps the magpie ran away from home?'

103

'Something strange is going on,' Jessie said, putting the golden grapes jewel into her pocket.

'Perhaps the magpie's nest is on the roof,' I said. 'And the jewel fell out and was blown into the tunnel by a really fierce wind.'

Jessie didn't answer. She was frowning and thinking.

'And perhaps . . . '

But Jessie wanted us to start climbing again.

I didn't dare say anything about jewels or magpies while we climbed. I tried not to think about it. I had a lot to try not to think about.

Without thinking about it, I decided I would hunt for the magpie's nest when we got on to the roof.

We went the direct route to the top. Jessie climbed alongside me, all the time showing me where to put my hands and feet. At the top, I hauled myself over the edge and Jessie followed.

I wanted to find the magpie's nest.

I didn't notice the person on the roof, at first.

She was standing as still as a statue. She was holding a pair of binoculars and gazing through them at the countryside. She was wearing a honey-coloured cloak.

Jessie found her voice before I found mine.

'I think we've discovered your magpie, Patrick,' she said.

Miss Fox lowered her binoculars. She turned slowly round to face us. I noticed she was wearing one gold earring. It was in the shape of a bunch of grapes.

She didn't look surprised to see us climbing on to the roof. She didn't try to hide. She just stood there as if she was seeing us and not seeing us all at the same time.

Then I noticed that she looked sad.

Jessie said, 'Miss Fox, I presume?'

Miss Fox just stared. But she didn't stare at us. She stared through us. Then she slowly turned and raised the binoculars to her eyes again and gazed out over the countryside.

'Someone's put a spell on her,' I whispered to Jessie. I don't know why, but I suddenly remembered the tooth fairy.

I shivered and shuddered.

'Miss Fox,' Jessie said in a strong, firm voice. 'What are you doing on my roof?'

'Trespassing,' said Miss Fox, without moving a muscle. She hardly even opened her lips. It was as though somebody else was speaking for her. Or through her.

'What's trespassing?' I asked Jessie in a weak, wobbly voice.

'Going on to someone's land without asking,' Jessie answered, without taking her eyes off Miss Fox. Then she said, 'Miss Fox is a person who calls a spade a spade. I like that.'

She sounded surprised.

I was surprised, too. I didn't hear Miss Fox say anything about spades. I knew she was someone who did a lot of digging.

Jessie asked Miss Fox how she happened to be on her roof.

Miss Fox said, 'I climbed your wall, of course. How else? It's a good wall. I'm interested in walls. And by the way' – she pointed to something down on the ground – 'I notice you have a bad drystone wall that needs repair. I can help you with that.'

I gulped.

Jessie went over to look.

Miss Fox and Jessie had a long talk about drystone walls. Miss Fox didn't mention the Romans. Jessie didn't mention the barbarians.

Then they had a long talk about climbing. Miss Fox was very interested in climbing.

'Do you like abseiling, too?' I said. I was looking forward to abseiling down.

But Miss Fox didn't answer me. She had a faraway look in her eyes. She started shaking her head slowly.

'I must apologize,' she said. 'I've made a dreadful mistake. This isn't the site I thought it was.'

'No Roman temple?' Jessie said cheerfully.

'No Roman temple,' Miss Fox said.

Jessie looked very happy. She didn't look a bit angry about Miss Fox. Jessie was a strange person. She was grinning from ear to ear.

'I told you so,' she told Miss Fox. 'I told you in my letter.'

Miss Fox nodded sadly.

'Cheer up.' Jessie held out the gold bunch of grapes. 'We found your earring.'

'Thank you,' Miss Fox replied. She took it and put it in her ear. 'This is very upsetting,' she said. She sounded very upset.

'We all make mistakes,' said Jessie.

'I don't,' said Miss Fox.

'My mum does,' I said.

'*Everybody* makes mistakes,' Jessie said, very firmly.

'My teacher, Miss Simms says . . . '

I was going to tell them about Miss Simms. I knew what Miss Simms would say when I told her about all my mum's mistakes. She would say, 'What did your mum learn from her mistakes, Patrick?'

But they didn't want to hear about Miss Simms. Jessie took Miss Fox's binoculars in a friendly sort of way, and said, 'Are you sure you made a mistake? Are you sure it isn't there? What are we looking for?'

'Tumuli.'

'What's tumuli?' I asked.

'Bumps,' Jessie said.

'What kind of bumps?'

'Bumps in the earth.'

Jessie put the binoculars to her eyes and had a good look. I tried to get a go, but she elbowed me off.

Miss Fox was muttering alongside me. 'It isn't a temple. It could be a midden, I suppose.'

'What's a midden?' I asked.

'A dung-heap,' Miss Fox said.

'What's a dung-heap?'

Miss Fox didn't answer. 'It's no good,' she said, suddenly getting red-faced and impatient and bad-tempered. 'The tumuli are wrong. All wrong.'

'A dung-heap is a place for chucking rubbish,' Jessie said to me. 'What's wrong with my bumps?' she said to Miss Fox, lowering the binoculars.

'They're not Roman.'

'What's so special about Roman bumps?'

'Only Roman tumuli are of any interest,' said Miss Fox, in a grand and mistake-making sort of way.

Jessie handed Miss Fox's binoculars back to her.

'I'll show you an interesting bump,' she said. 'Follow me.'

At Jessie's house nothing happened quite the way

you expected it. I followed Jessie and Miss Fox across the roof. They were talking at the tops of their voices, both at the same time. I couldn't tell if they were being friends or being enemies.

Then Jessie bent and picked up the abseiling gear.

Miss Fox put her hands on her hips.

'Well?' said Jessie. 'Do you accept the challenge?'

One of the things Jessie often said was: expect the unexpected. So I wasn't a bit surprised when Jessie held the sit harness up and Miss Fox climbed into it.

'What goes up must come down,' Jessie said sternly.

Miss Fox sniffed. 'Dear girl,' she said, in a superior sort of way, 'I've done more abseiling in my time than you've had hot dinners.'

'So you know what to expect?'

Miss Fox nodded. I could see she was expecting the unexpected.

Jessie grabbed hold of the bottom end of the sit harness and grabbed hold of the top end, and yanked the two together. Miss Fox doubled over, yowling.

'Good,' Jessie said.

She hooked the crab into both parts of the harness and tied Miss Fox up like a parcel. Then she looped the long red rope through the crab.

It was quite interesting watching Miss Fox abseiling down the side of Jessie's house.

Abseiling is like flying and swinging and swooping and sailing all at the same time.

It's very easy, but it looks very difficult.

It's quite safe, but it looks quite scary.

It should be smooth, but it can be bumpy.

Miss Fox abseiled down in a bumpy way and she landed with quite a bump in the garden.

10   Pot o' the Wall

Later, Miss Fox went back to her tent to write everything down and draw some pictures.

'I have to do it at once,' she said, sadly. 'Or I may make another mistake.'

Miss Fox opened her eyes wide when she said the word 'mistake', like a person looking at a ghost. Then she started blinking furiously.

And there was something else she had to do.

'I have to feed Augusta,' she explained.

'Who's Augusta?' I asked.

'Augusta comes everywhere with me,' Miss Fox answered. 'She's a very old, very fat, very bad-tempered tabby cat.'

'Oh,' I said.

Sam bristled. His tail twitched. Miss Fox looked at him and pulled her cloak around herself.

'Does Augusta go with you on the motorbike?' I said.

'Augusta comes with me everywhere.'

I stared hard at Miss Fox. I wondered if she knew she had made another mistake. 'Augusta didn't climb up the climbing wall with you,' I told her.

Miss Fox scowled.

Mum pulled a face.

'I wasn't being rude,' I said, before Mum could say anything.

But before Mum could say anything to me, Miss Fox said something to Mum. 'Are you a cat person?' she said.

Mum jumped. 'Not that sort of cat,' she said.

'Not that sort of person, I hope,' Dad said.

'People are cat people or dog people,' Miss Fox said firmly, giving Sam an unfriendly look.

We all watched her as she climbed over the stile and made her way across the field.

'Poor Miss Fox,' Mum said. 'I wish we could think of a way to cheer her up. It can't be very nice, making such a big mistake.'

We watched her getting smaller and smaller as she plodded across the fields to her tent. 'If only she could find something,' Mum said. 'That would cheer her up.'

'Find what?' Dad wasn't really paying attention. He was putting his boots on. They were clean and shiny.

'I don't know,' Mum said dreamily. 'Something.'

The hair at the back of my neck prickled.

'Something Roman,' Mum said.

My spine turned to ice.

Dad laced up his boots.

I tried to speak, but a lump like an ostrich egg filled my throat. Both my legs started jiggling and wiggling like busy tadpoles. The room was spinning slowly round and round. I reached out for a chair. I couldn't speak. I had to speak. What I had to say was wonderful.

'Wow!' I gasped, clutching the back of the chair.

But Mum and Dad were wandering out of the room, talking. They didn't see me. They didn't hear me.

'Jack!' I said. 'Wow! Listen! Jack!'

It was wonderful! It was true!

Jack wasn't listening. He was on his hands and knees near the back door. He was holding out a shred of lettuce. He was training Nero and some other woodlice to march together.

'Jack!.

I couldn't stand still. I started running round and round the chair, holding on to it in case I fell over.

'Be quiet,' Jack said. 'Keep still.' He had the woodlice nearly in a straight line. He waved the scrap of lettuce in front of them like a flag.

I fell to my knees. The woodlice scattered in every direction.

'Jack,' I cried. 'Listen. It's wonderful!'

Jack screeched at me in fury. 'You frightened them!'

'It's about Pot o'the Wall!'

'Come back!' Jack exclaimed, chasing a column of woodlice. 'Nero! Come here!'

The woodlice were going as fast as their legs would carry them, here and there all over the kitchen. They all looked exactly the same, like giant maggots in full armour.

'Jack!' I said. 'Listen. You can catch Nero later!'

Jack ignored me. He couldn't think of anything but Nero. But he couldn't decide which woodlouse was Nero. First he chased this one, then that. Sam helped.

I hopped from one foot to the other.

'There's Nero!' I said, pointing at one near my feet.

I couldn't fool Jack. He gave me a bitter, short look.

'Or there?' I said, pointing at another.

I couldn't get him to listen to the wonderful thing I had to tell him about Pot o'the Wall. I had to keep it locked up like a bubble waiting to burst inside me. It was wonderful. It was true.

'Wow!' I said to myself, 'Pot o'the Wall! Wow! Pot o'the Wall! Wow!'

Then I heard Mum's voice. She was shouting down the stairs from the top of the house. She was shouting from our attic bedroom.

'Patrick! Jack! Have you seen the state of your room? Come up here and sort out this rubbish heap at once! This instant!'

Mum didn't stop to listen. She said, 'I'm going to help Jessie fetch some supplies. Miss Fox is coming to dinner tonight. We won't be gone long. I want all this rubbish thoroughly tidied away by the time we get back.'

She was already on her way out.

Jessie was behind her. 'We'll be back in a tick,' she said. 'We'll be back in two shakes of a lamb's tail.'

I ran out after them.

'You leave those lamb's tails alone,' I shouted down the stairs after Jessie.

I would have shouted, 'Wait till I tell you about Pot o'the Wall!' But they were gone. The back door slammed. We heard the engine of Jessie's van. We heard the wheels on the gravel drive. Then everything went quiet.

Jack picked *Augustus Caesar's World* up from the floor where it was lying. He threw some stones and shells and pieces of bone off his bed. He stretched out, gave a deep sigh, and opened his book.

'I'm sorry about Nero,' I said.

Jack nodded.

'I expect you'll find another one like him.'

Jack shook his head. 'There won't be another one quite like Nero.'

I picked up Pot o'the Wall very gently. I ran my hand over his rough side. I felt his jagged edges. I knew.

'Jack?'

'What?' Jack wanted to read his book.

'Jack,' I said excitedly. 'When you went into the Roman Britain Living History Society, did you notice anything?'

'Of course I noticed something.'

'What?'

'All sorts of things.'

'Did you notice something in a glass case?'

Jack stared at me. 'Lots of things,' he said slowly.

'Did you notice something a bit like this?' I held out Pot o'the Wall.

'Yes.'

'Did you notice something with a label in front of it that said it was found by Miss Fox?'

Jack closed *Augustus Caesar's World*.

'You know what this is, don't you Jack?' The hairs on the back of my neck were prickling again. My spine was like ice. 'You know what it is, don't you?'

Jack touched the back of his neck. His hair must have been prickling, too.

'We've found it,' I said quietly.

Jack said, 'Wow!'

'We've found the other half of Miss Fox's cup,' I said.

Jack took Pot o'the Wall from me. He turned it over and over in his hands.

We both looked at it. We didn't say anything. Everything was quiet except for our breathing.

I said, 'I know it's the other half of Miss Fox's cup. I can tell by the jagged edges. I just didn't realize it before.'

'Of course it is,' Jack said.

'Wow!' we both said.

'We have to give it to her,' I said bravely. I knew that was what I had to do, but I was very, very sad when I thought of giving Pot o'the Wall away.

I knew I had to. I knew I couldn't keep him. Pot was Roman. He belonged with Miss Fox. Miss Fox would put him in a glass case. Perhaps someone would write a label with my name on it and the date in Latin. That would be nice. Or perhaps Miss Fox could get some superglue and stick the two bits of her cup together again.

Jessie said superglue was made out of sheep's ear wax. I wondered if Miss Fox knew.

I wondered if she would let Pot come and stay with me sometimes.

I was sad thinking all these things. I was quite

glad when Jack suddenly punched the pillow with his fist.

'No,' he said.

'No?'

'No.'

'No what?'

Jack was thinking hard. 'No. We won't *give* it to her,' he said. 'That won't cheer her up. She has to find it.'

'Find it? But where? It's already found.'

'We can put it back. Then we have to make sure Miss Fox goes to the exact place and finds it.'

That didn't sound like a very good idea to me.

'How can we be sure she'll find it?'

'We'll make sure she goes the exact same way you went.'

'I fell off a wall,' I said.

Jack frowned. 'I suppose we can't push her off the wall.'

We thought about that.

'Why not?' I said at last. I thought Miss Fox wouldn't mind being pushed off a little wall if it meant she found the other half of her cup.

I thought I wouldn't mind pushing Miss Fox off a little wall.

'The wall isn't there, stupid,' Jack cried. He gave me a friendly shove that sent me sprawling. 'You wrecked it. Remember?'

I didn't say anything. I picked myself up. I dusted myself off. I still wasn't sure that Jack's idea was a very good idea.

11   Caught in the Storm

We carried Pot o'the Wall very carefully up the steep field. We climbed over the fallen stones. A bunch of sheep watched us out of round, sheep's eyes.

We cleared a space near the big stone which had the funny squiggles on it. Once we started, we cleared a good big space. We decided Pot should have lots of space. We made sure he was sticking up nicely. Nobody could miss him.

Then we didn't know what to do.

We walked across the fields to our camp at Sam's Landing.

We pulled down some of our hut and started building a better one. We soon got tired of that.

'I hope Miss Fox will find Pot soon,' I said.

I wasn't happy about putting Pot back under the big stone.

We sat in the branches of the fallen trees. We threw pebbles into the river and thought of some ways to hurry Miss Fox up. She had to find Pot o'the Wall.

'I hope she'll find him before it gets dark,' I

said. It was already starting to get dark. A huge black cloud was climbing like a giant over the hill behind us.

I had a funny feeling about leaving Pot all alone in the steep field. But I was enjoying thinking up ways to help Miss Fox.

We had hundreds of ideas.

'We could kidnap the cat,' I suggested. 'And tie her in a sack. And leave her near the big stone. And Miss Fox would hear her miaowing. And go to the stone. And rescue the cat. And find Pot.'

Jack didn't like that idea. He had another one.

'We could write her a letter in code. And draw a map. And push it under her tent,' Jack said. 'When she's not looking.'

'We could put the letter and the map in the cat's basket.'

We went on like this for some time, thinking up so many good plans we couldn't decide which one to try first.

We spent a long time working out a secret code.

The giant crept closer. The sky darkened completely. A few drops of rain fell.

And then it happened. The sky ripped open. There was a flash, and then another, of pale green light. And, at exactly the same time, we heard a terrible booming and rolling and banging of thunder. The giant was coming towards us.

Pressed against the tree, I gripped the branch with both hands. I saw Jack's face. In the pale green flash of lightning he was deathly white. Sam started barking and splashing wildly in the shallows of the riverbank.

'What is it?' I cried.

Giant blobs of rain began falling.

We scrambled out of the tree. We splashed across the river. The water came up to our knees.

'The water's rising!' Jack yelled, as we clutched hold of clumps of grass to pull ourselves up a steep bank.

The rain started falling in sheets. Twigs and leaves on the river rushed by me. The river was boiling. It was boiling up and over like brown soup boiling everywhere.

In a second I was soaked. My hair was soaked. Water ran down my face and down my arms and down my legs. My clothes stuck to me. My shoes were like buckets. When I ran they made a squelching noise on the grass. My feet slithered and slid like wet fish on slabs.

'Come on,' Jack said.

Sam was ahead of us. We could hear him barking. We couldn't see him. All we could see was rain like a grey sheet hanging from the sky.

We ran. We slipped and slid. The rain fell on our heads in a steady stream.

'Miss Fox will get washed away!' I yelled. Rain splashed off my nose and in my eyes and mouth.

Jack didn't hear me. He was running with his head down and his arms up.

Then I thought of something else. Something terrible.

'Pot will get washed away!' I cried. 'Pot will get smashed and broken! We have to rescue Pot!'

Poor Pot. He was out in the rain, all alone. The rain was falling like a waterfall. The sky was like a bucket without any bottom.

We reached the house. As we stumbled up the drive, another sound caught my ears. It was a sound like thunder. BRMMMBRMMBRMM. BRM-MBRMMBRMM. Coming closer and closer, getting louder and louder. An engine.

'It's Jessie's van!' I shouted.

But it wasn't Jessie. The thunder exploded behind me. I tumbled into the soaking wet hedge.

Miss Fox roared by on her motorbike.

We all gathered in the porch, sheltering from the rain. It was driving into the ground like a hail of arrows.

All the fields were smudgy green. I could see the sheep, hunched in a bunch in a corner of the wall. I was glad I wasn't a sheep. They were a sorry sight.

Jack was a sorry sight, too.

Miss Fox was dressed in orange plastic from top to toe. She peeled it all off in the porch. Inside, she was completely dry.

I was completely wet. So was Jack. So was Sam. Huge puddles formed at our feet where we stood, panting and steaming, in the back porch.

'Miss Fox!' I cried. 'Something terrible has happened!'

Miss Fox said, 'Just a moment. I have to bring Augusta in.' She went out and fetched a basket wrapped in orange plastic. I could hear something hissing and spitting inside.

'Doesn't that dog have a shed?' she said, giving Sam another unfriendly look.

Sam stood dripping miserably.

'Miss Fox!' I exclaimed. 'A terrible thing has happened. Jack's made a terrible mistake. We've done something terrible!'

'Really?' said Miss Fox. She didn't seem surprised.

She fussed over Augusta. Augusta was very fat and not very nice.

Rain was pouring off the roof. Rain was filling the ditches. There were puddles everywhere. The river must be rising. It would burst its banks. Water would flood the land.

I knew we had made a terrible mistake.

'Miss Fox,' I said. 'Listen! It's Pot.'

'Pot?' said Miss Fox. 'Do you need a pot? At your age? How old are you, anyway?'

'Pot is out there!' I cried, flinging my arm wide to the open country. 'In the rain! Don't you understand?'

'I haven't a clue what you're talking about,' Miss Fox said.

Miss Fox picked Augusta out of the basket and stood holding and stroking her. Sam growled. Augusta hissed.

They didn't like each other.

'Augusta likes very few creatures,' Miss Fox said contentedly.

Sam planted his four feet wide. His head dropped. In a moment, he was nothing but a blur of shaking dog. A great wave of water flew from Sam and landed on Miss Fox and Augusta.

It was a long time before I could get Miss Fox to listen to me. But I had to tell her. She had to know. We had to rescue Pot o'the Wall before he was washed away for ever in the terrible storm. We had to get Pot. He was the other half of Miss Fox's cup!

'We have to go now!' I said.

Miss Fox looked at the windows and at the great globs of rain raining down them.

That was when Jessie appeared. Suddenly she was there in the doorway. Her eyes were bright and her cheeks were red and she was saying,

'Rain! Wonderful rain! I told you we needed rain!'

She started dancing about in the kitchen. She didn't seem to notice us all quietly dripping.

I told Jessie about Pot o'the Wall.

'He'll be washed away!' I cried. 'We'll never see him again. Miss Fox will never find the other half of her cup!'

A gleam appeared in Jessie's eye. 'Roman, you say? It fell out of the wall, you say?'

Miss Fox said, 'That's not surprising.' She looked annoyed. Perhaps she was annoyed about being wet. I thought she was probably annoyed that we found Pot o'the Wall before she did. Perhaps she was also annoyed that we put him back under the stone instead of keeping him in our nice, warm, safe, dry attic bedroom.

I wished we hadn't put Pot under the squiggly stone.

I wished we had kept him in our nice, warm, safe attic bedroom.

I wished we'd stayed there ourselves.

'We wanted to cheer you up,' I tried to explain. 'We wanted to let you find him.'

And now Pot was wet, and broken, and lost.

Miss Fox mouth went into a funny shape, like a raspberry. A sour raspberry. But she didn't take any notice of me. She talked to Jessie. 'The farmers in this part of the country,' she said, as if she was sucking a sour raspberry, 'are well known for breaking up old Roman roads to get stones for their drystone walls. We find many things mixed up with walls.'

'Do we?' Jessie said with a wicked smile.

'Yes,' said Miss Fox. 'Especially if the site is also the site of a midden.'

'Or a temple?' Jessie said, even more wickedly.

'We have to rescue Pot!' I cried.

'Of course we have to rescue Pot!' Jessie bounded across to Miss Fox and kidnapped her elbow. Before Miss Fox could protest, Jessie swept her through the back door. We all followed, except for Augusta, who took a flying fat leap out of Miss Fox's arms and landed in her dry basket.

It wasn't much fun getting soaking wet again.

As we trudged up towards the steep field, I kept my head down. I couldn't help noticing lots of pieces of pots that looked like Pot.

There were pots here and pots there. They were all honey-coloured and jagged at the edges. They were all dripping wet and sitting in puddles.

'All the rubbish was thrown on the midden,' Miss Fox said. 'We find wonderful finds of pots and shells and bones.'

We stood in the pouring rain beside the big

stone. I put my hand under it. The others stood and watched. There was nothing there. Pot o'the Wall was gone.

'Are you sure this is the right place?' Miss Fox said. She was looking at some other pieces of pot that were lying about. She kicked them with her toe. 'Broken flower pots,' she said. 'Rubbish.'

Jessie suddenly cried out. 'Just a minute!'

Jessie was standing stock still. Her mouth was open. Her eyes were goggling. She was goggling at the big squiggly stone.

'I don't believe it!' she breathed. 'It can't be!' she exclaimed.

She fell to the ground and started sweeping rubbish and small stones and rain water off the top of it.

'What is it?' I said. 'Is it Pot?'

'No,' Jessie said. 'No.'

She was clearing the top of the stone. She dug away some of the earth under it. It was a very big, flat stone. Now we could all see the top properly. It was covered in strange squiggles and round marks. It reminded me of something. Where had I seen marks like that before?

'Is it Roman?' Jack asked.

Miss Fox crouched down and peered at it, interested.

Jessie stoked the stone. 'It's much more interesting than that,' she said in an astonished

sort of way. 'It's a cup and ring stone. Look. It's astonishing. I knew there was one around here somewhere. I didn't know it was here.'

We all looked.

'Are you sure?' Miss Fox asked. 'I used to be very interested in cup and ring stones.' She leaned across Jessie. Their heads touched gently. Miss Fox's nose twitched. Her eyes started blinking very fast behind her spectacles.

Together, Jessie and Miss Fox scooped rain water out of the holes and cleared bits of things that sheep had done out of the squiggles. They were both very excited.

'I found it first,' I said.

'This is wonderful,' Jessie said. 'Wow! A cup and ring stone! Wow! What a find!'

'Will you put it in a glass case?' I asked her. 'With a label?' I was sad I wouldn't have my name on a label now that Pot was gone. I was sad that Pot was gone.

Jessie leapt to her feet, gave me a quick, rainy hug, and turned to the stone again. 'No, Patrick,' she said dreamily. 'A glass case isn't the right place for a cup and ring stone. This stone is staying right here. Where it belongs. Under the sky.'

She asked Miss Fox if she agreed.

Miss Fox agreed. 'Cup and ring stones are very special to this part of Yorkshire. They belong on the moors.'

I watched the rain filling up all the holes again.

'Imagine how old this stone is!' Jessie whispered.

'Older than the Romans,' Miss Fox said happily. 'I like to think a tired Roman legionary might have rested here, on his way to Hadrian's Wall perhaps.'

The strange thing was, Jessie liked to think that, too. She chatted happily to Miss Fox about cup and ring stones and the Romans, and Miss Fox chatted happily to Jessie about the Romans and cup and ring stones.

I thought about Pot. Perhaps he wouldn't have liked being in a glass case, either. Perhaps he was better off where he was, wherever that was. Somewhere under the sky. But I couldn't help wishing I could find him.

Jessie and Miss Fox walked back to the house arm in arm. The rain had stopped. The sun was shining. Everything gleamed and sparkled as if it had just been made.

Mum and Dad were walking across the field to meet us. Dinner was ready.

12   All Friends Together

'What a soggy saga!' Mum said, after we finished telling Mum and Dad what happened.

We were all sitting round the table having dinner. Everybody was dry. Everybody was hungry. Everybody was happy, except me. I couldn't help thinking about Pot o'the Wall, all alone somewhere under the sky.

I sneezed.

Then I sneezed again.

'Blow downwards, Patrick,' Dad said, giving me a pink paper napkin.

Miss Fox and Jessie were friends now.

Mum said, 'It's so lovely when your friends make friends with each other.'

I sneezed again. I was thinking sadly about Pot o'the Wall. Poor Pot. He had lost his friends. He was all alone somewhere where his friends couldn't find him.

'Look.' Jack nudged me. He had a woodlouse friend in a matchbox in his lap. I had Big Dog. Not in a matchbox. 'Did you know,' Jack said, 'a woodlouse's shell is stronger than bone?'

Miss Fox's eyes brightened. They glimmered and glittered and glinted behind her spectacles. 'That's all very well,' she said, leaning across me to tap Jack on the arm. 'But what about the octopus in the sewers of ancient Rome?'

Dad said, 'Don't you mean octopi? If it's more than one octopus? That's correct Latin, I believe.'

'Miss Fox wouldn't make a mistake about something like that, darling,' Mum said.

'What octopus?' Jack asked.

'The octopus and the barrel of fish sauce!' exclaimed Miss Fox.

Jack's face lit up. 'Oh, *that* octopus!'

'You must know the story.'

Jack knew the story.

'Once upon a time . . . ' Jessie said happily, leaning back in her chair and folding her arms.

Jack and Miss Fox both tried to tell the story, but Miss Fox won. 'A Roman merchant couldn't work out who was eating the fish sauce in his cellar,' she began. 'So he put a slave on guard duty. One night, the astonished slave saw an octopus crawl out of the sewers and into the cellar. The octopus prised the lid off the barrel of fish sauce. He then ate the entire contents. The slave was too amazed to do anything!'

'The octopus was foraging!' Jack cried.

'Poor fish,' I said.

'Strong octopus,' said Dad.

'Piffle!' said Jessie. 'I don't believe a word of it.'

Jack and Miss Fox started taking it in turns to tell stories about the Romans. Some of them were funny. Some of them were piffle. I was surprised they could forget about Pot o'the Wall so easily.

I listened for a bit. Then I tucked Big Dog under my arm and slipped down from my chair. I went out the back door.

Everybody else might forget about Pot o'the Wall, but I couldn't. Perhaps my mum thought he was rubbish. I knew he wasn't. He was a friend. He was the other half of Miss Fox's pot and I was determined to find him.

I set off across the field. Halfway up, I heard a familiar noise behind me. I looked round. Running from the house, all blurred and shimmery in the golden light, were two figures. Jack and Sam.

'Wait for us,' Jack called.

I waited.

'We have to find Pot,' Jack said, looking up at the sky. 'There's still some daylight left.'

I didn't remind Jack that it was his idea to put poor Pot back under the stone. I was sneezing too much for one thing. For another, I was glad he was with me. There wasn't much time. Already, the sky was turning from gold to orange. The sun was sinking lower and lower. I knew what that meant. Soon it would be dark. Then it would be pitch black.

We scrambled up the field as fast as we could. When we got to the drystone wall, we went more slowly, carefully looking around us for clues.

At the cup and ring stone, we both got down on our hands and knees and crawled all round it, picking up tufts of grass and shifting little piles of rubbish and rocks that had once been a wall. There was no sign of Pot.

'It's hopeless,' Jack said, sitting on the stone.

'Wait!' I cried. 'Look!'

I pushed Jack off the cup and ring stone. 'Look at the pattern on the stone,' I said. 'Why didn't we notice it before?'

Jack couldn't see what I could see.

'It's like an arrow!' I cried. 'Look!'

There was no doubt about it. If you looked at it in the right way, which was sideways, the markings on the stone made a shape that was a bit like a sort of arrow. And the arrow was pointing towards the setting sun.

'It's a message,' I said solemnly.

Jack put his head on one side and screwed up his eyes. He couldn't see what I could see. 'Well,' he said. 'Perhaps. Maybe.'

'Definitely,' I said. 'A message about Pot.'

'How can it be a message about Pot?' Jack cried. 'We only lost Pot today, and this stone has been here for thousands of years!'

I didn't bother to answer. I was following the path of the arrow. I went very carefully, looking this way and that, keeping in a straight line, picking my way through rock and grass, thistles and thorns, sheep bits and cowpats. I had to hold my hand over my eyes to cut out the sun which was shining right at me. On the ground, even under the shade of my hand, everything looked orangey-ish.

Except for one thing. It was tucked under a clump of thistles, beside a jumble of rock. It was dusty honey-coloured, with jagged edges.

'Pot!' I cried. I ran forward and pulled him out.

It was the same old Pot, same rough surfaces, same jagged edges. I couldn't see any new scratches or marks. Pot was safe. I'd known I would find him.

Jack and Sam came up and we took turns holding Pot and saying how happy we were. Pot was back.

'Now we can show him to Miss Fox and *prove* he's Roman!' Jack cried.

I looked up. All the sky had darkened to a deep pink. The sun, a red ball, was low down behind the trees. Long shadows stretched across the field. I heard voices.

Mum and Dad and Jessie and Miss Fox were out in Jessie's garden.

'Come on!' Jack said. 'What are you waiting for? We've found Pot!'

Before I could answer, Jack swept Pot out of my hands. Before I could stop him, he was off, clutching Pot and running towards the house as fast as his legs would carry him.

It was no use crying out. I didn't even chase after Jack. Something held me back.

I was happy to find Pot, but I was sad about something too. Pot o'the Wall was Roman. A Roman pot would have to go and live in a glass case at the Roman Britain Living History Society. But I was sure that Pot was like me, and would much rather stay in Yorkshire.

Mum waved to me from the garden. It was so dark by now that I could only just see her. Everybody else was crowded in a little huddle around Jack.

'Darling!' Mum said excitedly. 'Imagine! You were right! That piece of old pot you picked up, it *is* Roman. Miss Fox said so.'

'Oh,' I said sadly. 'That's nice.'

'Aren't you pleased?' She looked at me, puzzled. 'You were right.'

'I know,' I said, still feeling sad.

'What's the matter, Patrick?'

At first I said nothing was the matter, then I said everything was the matter, and then I told her about not wanting to let Pot be put in a glass case so far away from where he belonged. 'But if he's the other half of Miss Fox's pot, I'll have to,' I blubbered. 'And if he's Roman, I'll have to. And I don't want to.'

I didn't realize Jessie was standing behind me. She put her arms around me. 'What's all this?' she said. 'Haven't you forgotten something?' She whispered in my ear.

Then Miss Fox came up with Pot o'the Wall in her hands and Jack beside her. She was smiling and blinking happily. 'Late Roman,' she said. 'Romano-British. Local workmanship. Rather poor, really. An interesting find, however.'

'How interesting?' I asked quietly.

'*Very* interesting,' Jessie said quickly. 'In fact, if Miss Fox is right about the midden, there should be some other interesting finds to be found.'

'Undoubtedly,' said Miss Fox, and started telling everybody all the interesting things people found on Roman rubbish heaps.

'Oh,' I said. Then I whispered to Jessie, 'But you said . . . '

'Yes,' Jessie whispered back. 'It's my land.'

Jessie suddenly clapped her hands, just like a teacher when she wants everyone to stop what they're doing and pay attention.

Jack hissed at me, 'It's not the other half of Miss Fox's pot, silly.'

'But it is Roman.'

'I told you that,' Jack said.

'I found it,' I reminded him.

'I found it first,' he said.

'And you lost it.'

This went on for a little while.

'If Miss Fox wants to dig up the midden,' Jessie was saying, 'I'm happy to help her, on one condition.'

Jessie's condition was a good one. Miss Fox could dig in Jessie's garden, but if she found anything, it had to stay in Jessie's house.

Jessie had decided to have a little history display at the Centre. She would get some glass cases, and make some labels. If Miss Fox found some interesting things, everybody in Yorkshire would be able to look at them. Anybody who came to the Centre would be able to think about Romans, *and* about the ancient Yorkshire people.

'And afterwards, they'll be able to go out into the field and look at the cup and ring stone,' Miss Fox added, quite happy with Jessie's condition.

'What about Pot o'the Wall?' Jack said.

That was what I had been wondering, but I didn't dare say.

Jessie turned to me. 'What about him, Patrick? What do you think? You found him.'

'*I* found him,' said Jack.

I didn't need to think. 'He should stay here,' I said firmly. 'This is where Pot belongs.'

'Good,' Jessie said, giving me a big hug.

'Good,' Mum and Dad said.

'Good,' said Miss Fox.

'Now,' said Dad, taking a folded map out of the back pocket of his jeans and holding it up in the darkness. 'Remember?'

'Hadrian's Wall!' Mum and Jack both cried out together.

'Hadrian's Wall!' I started saying, but the words got caught up with a huge sneeze. What I actually said was, 'Hadri-at-tish-ooall!'

When I tried to speak again, I couldn't find my voice at all.

'Dear me!' Mum cried. 'You sound like a sheep with a sore throat.'

'That boy's got the flu,' Miss Fox said, as if it wasn't something she ever had anything to do with.

Everybody agreed I should be put to bed with a hot water bottle and a drink of hot milk with lots of honey and a little bit of lemon in it.

'And when Patrick's better,' Jessie said, 'why don't we *all* go to Hadrian's Wall?'

'And Sam?' Jack said quickly.

'Of course,' said Jessie.

'And Augusta?' That was Miss Fox.

Nobody was very interested in Augusta going to Hadrian's Wall.

Suddenly I started feeling very sleepy. Dad

picked me up. 'Look at the sky,' he said.

I looked. It was stuffed with stars.

Miss Fox pulled her cloak around her. She said, 'Out here, under the sky like this, you can imagine being a Roman soldier, marching, fighting, foraging, freezing, dreaming of warm nights in Rome.'

'Out here,' Jessie said, 'under this sky, you can imagine anything.'

I rested my head on my dad's shoulder. All I could imagine was hot water bottles and hot milk and hot honey and warm beds.

'How heavy am I?' I asked my dad sleepily.

'Heavier than Hadrian's Wall,' he said.

Other titles by Norma Clarke

PATRICK IN PERSON

'Are you saying,' Jack said, as we all went indoors, 'that you absolutely won't ever let me have a dog? Absolutely no? Never? Is that what you're saying?'

Patrick and his older brother Jack love animals – but their parents object to pets in town. Patrick is a vegetarian; he is also athletic and wants to be an actor – but above all he is a defender of human and animal rights. With wry humour and a dogged sense of justice, he describes the family's unforgettable summer holiday in Yorkshire when he fights for the equality of all – children, dogs and even nits – and Jack, at last, gets a dog to care for.

'*Patrick in Person* by Norma Clarke is that welcome rarity, a genuinely funny book.' *Observer*

THEO'S TIME

Theo's family think that his problem is that he is bad at maths. But Theo thinks that the real problem is having extra maths lessons – until he goes to Mrs Gordon's. Astonishing, and often frightening, it becomes the most exciting time of Theo's life – new friends, enemies, problems, solutions and all.

'Norma Clarke's writing has a wonderful lightness of touch, an incisive ability to point up the absurdity of adults against the reassuring normal oddities of children.' *Sunday Telegraph*